I0517075

BIKER'S GIRL

by

LIA ANDERSSEN

Published by **CHIMERA**
ISBN 9781780804682

Chapter 1
The Watchman

The girl stood alone figure by the wide river. She wore a short summer dress, creased and stained after many nights of being slept in. She was a picture of young beauty, her neck slim and graceful and her face, with its slightly pouting mouth and pert nose, was framed by brown tresses of hair that hung to below her shoulders. But it was her eyes that men always noticed first. Brown and almond shaped, they had a wide innocence about them that made her seem supremely vulnerable, the long curling lashes fluttering in a manner that made her seem at the same time alluring and guileless.

She surveyed the scene before her. The banks of the river were steep and precarious, and she realised she would not be able to reach its waters from where she was. She began to search for somewhere that would give her safe access.

She followed its edge for some distance, occasionally having to take detours inland to avoid the dense vegetation that grew alongside it. At last she found a spot where the bank had crumbled and she was able to climb down to the water. She placed her bundle carefully beneath a bush, kicked off her dusty shoes and scrambled down to the water's edge. It was shallow at the edges and she stepped in, the delicious cool of the water like balm on her tired feet.

She remained there for some time, splashing with her hands and feet and wetting her face with the refreshing water. She scooped handfuls up and drank it gratefully. She strode in deeper until she had to lift the hem of her dress to avoid wetting it.

What she really desired though, was to immerse herself completely. Did she dare do it here? She looked around. The spot she was in was quite secluded, surrounded by trees and bushes. Besides, she doubted that anyone would be about in such a place.

In a moment she had decided. Reaching behind her she took hold of the zipper on her dress and slid it down to her waist. She wriggled out of the garment, and stood in only her bra and briefs. Taking a further surreptitious glance about her she unclipped the bra, sliding it down her arms and tossing it aside. Her young breasts were firm and beautifully formed, the brown nipples upturned.

She hooked her thumbs into her pants and slipped them down with a single graceful movement. She tossed them aside and stood for a moment, magnificent in her nakedness, her sex prominent in its triangle of dark pubic hair, her curvaceous rear now fully revealed. She ran her hands over her skin, enjoying its silky feel beneath her fingers.

She hesitated for a moment, then in a sudden concession to modesty she pulled a small cloth from the bundle, wrapping it round her so that it just barely concealed her below the waist. Then she stepped down the bank again and slid into the cold water, allowing it to cover her legs and lap about her thighs.

A movement in the grass beside her caught her eye and she gave a sudden scream, the sound stifled almost as soon as it left her lips. She stared at the spot on the river bank. Surely it couldn't have been a rat? A water rat? Of all things there was nothing she feared more than rats, ever since the dreadful beast she had encountered in the woodshed when she was very young.

The grass moved again, then to her relief a blackbird hopped out, gazing inquisitively about. But the fright had been enough to take her thoughts back to who she was, and why she was here.

The girl's name was Lia, and she was running away. Although she knew what she was running from, she was unsure where she was running to. She just knew that she had to escape, to leave her former existence behind her and search for a new life.

She had been brought up in the City. Abandoned at birth by her unknown parents she had drifted from orphanage to orphanage in an unhappy childhood. At sixteen she had been given the opportunity to leave the dreary institutions of her youth in order to work in a clothing factory, long hours of sewing during the day, evenings spent in a depressing hostel watching TV or just sitting alone in her room, gazing at the wall.

As with many of the manufacturing companies in those days of homelessness, she lived in a works-owned hostel, obeying its rules and curfews in order to hold on to her job.

Jobs and homes had been at a premium for many years now, and it was this factor that had been the main cause of the breakdown in law and order that had finally occurred. The cities had become fortresses, high walls and fences surrounding them, entry strictly controlled. Inside the boundaries they were places of fear, the gangs that roamed the streets barely under the control of the Police Forces who patrolled high above in their helicopters, cars and foot patrols having long since become unsafe. The inhabitants of the cities now led a troglodyte existence, travelling the short distance to work via subways, purchasing what they could get from the small stores within their places of work.

It was from this that Lia had escaped. The colourlessness, the darkness of the buildings and subways, the drudgery of the days followed by the tedium of the nights.

The final straw had been the watchman.

Each hostel had its watchman, waiting in blue uniform and peaked cap in the small office near the entrance, checking identity cards before admitting anyone, locking the heavy steel doors at nine o'clock every night, supervising the extinguishing of lights at ten thirty, carrying out the everyday tasks in the building such as repairing leaks or changing lightbulbs.

The watchman in Lia's hostel was called Mick. In his middle thirties, his head shaved, his arms heavily tattooed, he was obsessed with bodybuilding and his every spare moment was spent lifting weights or exercising on the equipment that filled his room.

It was some time before Lia had noticed that he was taking a particular interest in her. He would spend ages examining her pass., studying the photo and then looking her up and down, his eyes so penetrating that she found herself unable to meet them. When they encountered one another in the narrow corridors of the hostel he would make no attempt to let her by, so she would have to press against him in order to pass. In the evening, if she was in the television room he would come and sit beside her, his leg rubbing against hers, laughing loudly at the antics on the screen.

He began prowling about outside her room at night, so that she feared to go out, and sometimes, when she returned from work, she was sure he had been in her room, searching through her drawers, examining her underwear.

But it was the incident with the rat that brought matters to a head.

She returned to her room late one evening, after the lights had been extinguished. She was used to groping her way down those long narrow hallways in the dark and found the door easily. She slipped inside, closing the door behind her, then stripped off all her clothes, dropping them in the laundry basket. Rummaging in a bottom drawer she pulled out an old T-shirt and dragged it over her head. It was large, stretched with continuous washings so that the neck hung wide, exposing her left shoulder, its hem barely reaching her thighs, so she had to pull it down to preserve her modesty.

She had climbed wearily into bed and lain in the darkness, letting her mind wander before dropping off to sleep.

Lia would never know precisely what woke her, but the more she thought about it the more she wondered if it was the sound of the door to her room clicking shut.

She lay on the bed, her eyes open, suddenly wide awake. It was then that she heard it; a faint scratching sound coming from the end of the bed. She slipped gently from between the sheets, then stood for a second, holding her breath. There it was again! Reaching for her bedside table she slid open a drawer and withdrew the small flashlight, kept there for emergencies. She approached the bed apprehensively, afraid of what she might see. She hesitated for a moment, steeling her nerves, then switched it on.

The rat was enormous, its body at least ten inches long, its wiry tail stretching out behind. Its fur was grey, with brown blotches caused by some sort of mange. Its eyes were dark and evil, and it crouched on the bed baring its teeth.

Lia screamed and dropped the flashlight. It clattered to the floor and went out, plunging the room into darkness once again. She backed towards the door, a primeval panic overtaking her as she groped for the handle. Her fingers scrabbled with it, unable to make it turn. At last she regained control of her shaking hands enough to release it. She twisted the handle and then she was out, slamming the door behind her, fighting down the feelings of fear and nausea that threatened to engulf her.

She stood for some time, leaning against the door, waiting until her breathing became more controlled. Her hands shook violently and her legs felt weak. It was the most horrible thing she had ever seen. She had to get rid of it. She began to think what she could do, where she could go for help. The hostel was quiet, the doors all locked. She couldn't rouse anyone at this time of night. There seemed no alternative; she would have to find the watchman.

She groped her way back down the corridors towards the entrance to the building, descending the dark staircase to the lobby. The watchman's room was just off the main hallway and she could see a light shining beneath the door. She hesitated for a moment at the threshold, then knocked.

"Who is it?"

"Number seventeen." She was reluctant to use her name with him.

There was a short silence, then the handle turned and the door swung open. He stood in the doorway, in shorts and an open shirt. Beads of sweat showed on his forehead and she guessed he had been exercising. He smiled when he saw it was her, baring his uneven teeth. "Come in," he said.

Lia stepped past him into the room. She had glimpsed its interior through the doorway before but had never been inside. As she glanced around she began to feel uncomfortable. Everywhere the room betrayed its occupant's maleness. A sturdy rifle cabinet stood by the door, the weapons inside gleaming, whilst all about the floor were weights and exercise equipment. A bed stood unmade in the corner with magazines strewn on and around, a mixture of hardcore pornography, guns and body building titles. On the walls were photos of women, all naked and in all kinds of poses, some of them bound or chained, many of them being penetrated by the stiff penises of muscular men, nothing at all left to the imagination. As she gazed about she heard the watchman close the door behind her, followed by the unmistakeable sound of a bolt being shot across. She began to wish she had not come.

She turned to face him. He was smiling slightly, his eyes roaming up and down her body. She shivered, realising for the first time the inadequacy of the T-shirt in conserving her modesty. She tugged at the hem, causing her left breast to be exposed almost to the nipple. She released the hem quickly and the material rode up her thigh again. He grinned, enjoying her embarrassment.

"What's the problem?" he said at last.

"A rat. There's a rat in my room."

"Number seventeen?" he asked unnecessarily.

"Yes."

"What sort of rat?"

"I don't know. A grey one. All I know is it's in my room."

"Need the exterminators. They deal with rats. Not my job, rats. Call the exterminators in the morning."

"In the morning?" she cried in dismay. "But what can I do until then?"

He shrugged.

She stood for a moment, thoroughly ill at ease, her hands still tugging at the hem of the T-shirt, wishing she had put on some underwear. "Isn't there somewhere else I can sleep for tonight?" she asked at last.

The man glanced pointedly across at the bed in the corner, then back at her. She blushed. "Another room I meant," she muttered.

"All the rooms are full, you know that."

She had an inspiration. "Can I sleep in the TV room?"

He shook his head. "Against the rules. TV room's locked up for the night."

"But the rat! Can't you do something about it?"

"Not my job," he repeated. "Not worth my while, chasing rats."

She stood silent again, trying to think. She knew that nothing on earth would persuade her to re-enter the room as long as the creature was in there. But she also knew there was nowhere else to go. She looked at him. She had a little money saved, perhaps that would help.

"What if I made it worth your while?"

He smiled slightly. "Maybe we could talk about that." He turned and crossed the room to where an ancient fridge was rattling quietly, opened it and took out two cans.

"Beer?" he asked, and without waiting for a reply tossed one of the cans to her. The throw was deliberately high and, without thinking, she reached both hands above her head to catch it. As she did so the T-shirt rode up, momentarily exposing the dark triangle of her pubic hair to him. He watched as she dragged the hem back down, glowing with embarrassment.

"Sit down," he said, indicating a small hard-backed chair in the centre of the room. She hesitated, glancing back at the bolted door behind her. There seemed nothing else for it. She sat gingerly down, trying to pull the hem of the T-shirt over her bottom. She pressed her legs tightly together, tucking the front of the shirt into the gap at the top of her legs. She felt the material pull downwards, exposing a generous expanse of cleavage. She opened the beer and began sipping it.

"You like to work out?" he asked. She shook her head.

"You should, it's good for you." She smiled bleakly.

"You like to try some of my equipment? I could put you through a proper workout. Ten minutes on the rowing machine, ten on the bike and then maybe some weightlifting."

"Maybe some other time."

"I thought maybe now."

"I, er, not at the moment," she replied, feeling more uncomfortable than ever.

"I thought maybe you could go through a routine, then I could go kill that rat."

"Some other time."

He shrugged. "Suit yourself. Maybe I'll kill the rat some other time." He stood up suddenly, his mood changed. "Meanwhile you have to go back to your room." His voice had become remote and officious. "It's the rules."

"But you said..."

"I said we'd talk about it. Well, we've talked, and we don't seem to have agreed."

She stared at him, her mind reeling. So that was it. It wasn't money he wanted after all. What he wanted was to feast his eyes on her barely dressed body while she performed for him. To watch her work out on his machines. But she was so inadequately dressed. How could she possibly hope to retain her modesty on any of them in a T-shirt that even now was threatening to expose her most private parts? And even if she did, the question was, would it stop at that? And what if it didn't? So far her experience of sex had involved little more than surreptitious fumbling at the back of the cinema, and a brief and unsuccessful encounter with a boy from work who had taken her virginity in the men's toilet, and left her frustrated and ashamed.

The trouble was, there was no alternative. She knew she couldn't return to her room with the rat still in there. The thought of the rodent crouching on her bed made her feel physically sick. She glanced at the photos on the wall again. Perhaps he just liked to watch. Perhaps she would be OK.

She eyed him over the top of the beer can. "Just a workout?" she said. "And then you'll kill the rat?"

He grinned. "Promise," he said.

"Have... have you got some shorts I could wear?"

"What, in my size?"

"Perhaps I should go and get some."

"From your room? Be careful of that rat."

She could see he was enjoying himself. It was the T-shirt or nothing. Lia took a long swig at the beer, then placed it on the floor and stood up. "Where do I start?"

"The rowing machine. Ten minutes on that."

She eyed the contraption. It consisted of a square leather seat which slid back and forth on rails. At one end were footrests, and the two 'oars' projected on either side. She stepped between the rails and lowered herself onto the seat, still straining to keep the hem of the shirt down. Once in position she placed her feet on the footrests and grasped the oars.

"Right," he said. He had produced an electronic timer from somewhere and set it on the chair. He fiddled with it briefly, then turned to her. "Ten minutes," he said, pressing a button. The numbers on the dial began to flash in a reducing sequence.

Lia pulled on the oars. They pivoted backwards and the seat slid forward, forcing her to bend her knees. Then she pushed and the seat returned to its original position. She pulled again and the motion was repeated. She found that, with some difficulty, she was able to keep her knees together, though she knew that as she came to a momentary halt at the end of each stroke she was affording him a brief glimpse of her sex, so she rowed harder, trying to stay on the move and continuing to hold her legs tightly together.

She rowed on, finding a rhythm and timing her breathing with the strokes. The effort was beginning to tire her and she felt herself starting to sweat. Her breasts pressed against the fabric of the shirt as she stretched, and she saw he was watching them with some enjoyment. The time on the clock ticked away as she rowed, back and forth, back and forth, her eyes closed now, her forehead beginning to glisten with the effort.

At last there was a buzz from the timer and she knew the ten minutes were up. She sat for a short time, regaining her breath, slumped forward on the seat. She had come through the first part of the ordeal reasonably well, she thought. She looked up at him.

"What next?"

"The exercise bike I think."

She climbed to her feet, breathing heavily. The shirt was beginning to stick to her body with the sweat, emphasising the shape of her breasts.

The bike stood in one corner, all gleaming chrome with a large crank and a thin leather saddle. He climbed on, showing her how to sit and how to set the tension on the crank. "Just a smooth ride first," he said, slackening it off. Then he stood back, watching her expectantly.

Gingerly she stepped over the centre of the machine and hoisted herself up onto the thin saddle. It was set high for his own convenience and she felt exposed sitting astride it. She tried to pull the shirt down over her bottom again and to tuck it between her legs.

"OK," he said, "away you go."

Lia put her feet up on the pedals and began to turn them.

It was harder than she had expected, and she found herself leaning forward and pushing hard. As she did so the T-shirt sprang out from under her bottom and rode up her thighs so that her bum was half exposed and a little of her pubic hair peeped out from beneath. The man grinned happily.

"That's better," he said. "You seem to be getting the hang of it now."

Lia reddened with embarrassment, aware of her predicament, and equally aware that she was helpless to do anything about it.

She rode on, developing a rhythm. Her feet pedalled hard and she began to work up a sweat once again. Her breasts trembled as she pedalled, clearly outlined beneath the T-shirt. The shirt rode higher, revealing her nether lips astride the thin saddle. As she strained, the leather ridge of the seat as it rubbed against her naked sex began to stir unexpected emotions. She felt a wetness as the constant motion teased her clitoris into life. She found herself bearing down hard on the saddle, and moving her hips back and forth in a new rhythm not entirely connected with the cycling.

8

She tried hard to constrain the feeling that was welling up inside her. She concentrated on the clock. Two minutes to go. She forced herself to think of other things; of her work, the TV show she had watched that night, but all the time her body was thrusting down on that thin ridge of leather. She looked up and saw he was watching her closely. She wondered if he was aware of her stimulation. Then she looked down and realised the saddle was glistening with moisture, and she knew he could see it too. She checked the clock. One more minute. She must hold out for one more minute. She mustn't let herself be overcome while he watched.

On she pedalled. The seat was becoming slippery as her wetness increased. Once again she felt her passion threatening to overwhelm her as the hard leather stimulated her between her legs. She could feel her sex lips and clitoris swelling with her ardour and her nipples had come erect beneath the T-shirt so that they projected proudly, clearly visible through the increasingly damp garment. The shirt was riding up almost to her waist, revealing the delicious pink globes of her arse to her lone audience.

The clock continued to tick the time away and she pedalled on, breathing heavily, her eyes closed, trying desperately to fight down her desire. The seconds seemed like minutes. Would she never be able to stop? Then the buzz sounded and she ceased pedalling gratefully, though she found herself momentarily unable to control her hips, which were still moving her sex back and forth over the ridge of leather.

With an enormous effort of will she lifted herself from the saddle and climbed from the bike. She stood beside it, panting with the exertion and with the vestiges of lust.

He came across and examined the machine. He ran his finger over the saddle. It came off wet. He held it up to her and grinned.

"Enjoy that, did you?"

Lia reddened, and realising the shirt was still around her waist she yanked it down clumsily. "What now?" she asked.

"The weights." He indicated the machine; a padded bench with a device at one end made up of wires and pulleys attached to a series of weights. Hanging above the bench was a chrome bar with rubber handgrips. Lia sat on the edge of the bench, then swung her legs up and lay back.

"Just one thing," he said. "You need the wristbands."

She looked at him, puzzled. "What wristbands?"

"These." He showed her two leather bands, with chrome rings attached. The rings came apart with some sort of catch. "Hold out your arms."

She obeyed, still slightly puzzled, and he snapped on the bands, first one wrist then the other, fastening them tight around her wrists with a click.

"Now grasp the bar."

She reached up, taking hold of the handgrips. Snap! Snap! Before she realised what he was doing he had clipped the rings around the bar, on the outside of the grips. Too late she saw she'd been tricked. Even before she could cry out he had hold of her right ankle, pulling it down to the floor. She began trying to kick free, but he was too strong for her. From his pocket he produced a reel of sticky tape and bound her leg to the chrome support of the bench. Then he took hold of her other leg, gripped it hard and yanked it over the edge of the seat, where he secured it in a similar way. Then he stood back to admire his handiwork.

The girl was trapped and helpless, her arms stretched wide apart above her head, her body pulled tight by the bonds on her ankles. The T-shirt was once again riding up, exposing her open sex. She stared at him fearfully. What a fool she'd been to fall for the trick with the wristbands. Now she was really in trouble.

He crossed the room to a small chest of drawers. He rummaged in a drawer, then pulled out a knife. It was a large hunting knife with a long curved blade serrated towards the tip. The handle was made of some kind of animal horn, about nine inches long and itself curved. It was the most wicked looking weapon she had ever seen. He weighed the instrument in his hand, as if handling it for the first time. Then holding it in front of him, the blade pointing upward, he approached her.

She shrank back in fear at the sight of the blade so close to her. He brought it down and let its cold steel touch her thigh. She shivered as he grinned at her discomfort. Then he grabbed the hem of the shirt and began slicing through the material. The knife was sharp and made easy work of the thin garment, sliding up to the neck which he cut with a single jerk, so that the two halves sprang apart, revealing Lia's breasts. Then just as easily he sliced from sleeve to neck on both sides. He pulled the ragged remains from under her and tossed them aside, then returned and stood at the foot of the bench admiring his captive.

Lia presented a delightful sight, her hands held high, emphasising her vulnerability. Her breasts, firm and young, were parted slightly, making a narrow valley between them, the dark nipples forming prominent peaks. Her belly was flat, her pubic hair neatly trimmed to a dark triangle. Her slim legs were forced brutally apart, revealing her open sex to him, as if in invitation.

He moved to her side, placing his hand flat on her stomach. She wriggled slightly, staring fearfully up at him. His hand moved up to her breast.

"Don't!" she pleaded.

He grinned. His hand cupped the underside of her breast, enjoying its smooth softness. He worked it round, feeling the nipple, rubbing it between his coarse fingers.

Almost at once the nipple began to harden as the girl responded to his touch. She closed her eyes, wishing her body would obey her. His other hand was on the other breast now and she felt that respond to him as well. Despite herself she found her body reacting to his caresses.

He continued the stimulation, squeezing and kneading her pliant breasts while his captive writhed beneath him. He leant over and began sucking one of her nipples, which stood hard and proud, inviting his lips. She groaned aloud as she felt his mouth close over it, sucking hard, his tongue flicking at the tip while his fingers continued to work on the other.

He lifted his head from her and looked her in the eye. "Like that, don't you?" Lia closed her eyes, ashamed.

His mouth returned to her nipple, but she felt his hand leave her other breast and begin sliding down across her ribcage, over her stomach and down towards her sex.

"No!" she said, struggling hopelessly.

But the hand continued its journey, pausing slightly to stroke her pubic hair, and then down between her legs, sliding between the outer lips of her vagina and finding her swollen love bud almost at once.

She let out a gasp of passion as she felt him take it between his fingers. A warm wetness rose within her as he toyed with her, teasing her clitoris. His fingers stroked round it with a circular motion, barely touching, making her cry out in frustration.

"No," she said again, but her aroused body was saying the opposite. She flung her head from side to side as he continued to suck and tease. She felt her juices running freely. She knew she would soon be unable to contain them and she blushed with shame at the thought of him seeing this blatant betrayal of her arousal.

He moved down the bench so he was sitting between her open thighs, studying her wet pink cleft, pulling apart the lips and increasing her exposure still further. He reached for the knife, which he had left lying on the bench, and she watched with apprehension as he stroked its handle suggestively, still studying her naked body.

He ran the hilt of the knife up the inside of her thighs, its coldness against her skin making her shiver. He pressed it harder to her flesh, sliding it ever further up towards the top of her legs. She groaned with the feel of it, wondering what he would do next.

The handle of the knife was thick and gnarled, about an inch in diameter, curving to a rough knob on its end. He held it by the blade in his right hand whilst easing apart the lips of her sex with the other. Then, slowly, he began pushing the handle against them, twisting as he pushed.

With a gasp of uncontrolled lust she felt it enter her vagina, its coldness causing the muscles to contract, almost pushing it out again. But he held hard to the instrument and began gently pressing it further in, continuing to twist it as he did so, so that the friction stimulated her deliciously.

Further and further he pushed. Lia, now completely out of control, strained to widen her legs still further to accommodate the makeshift dildo that was working her up to such a frenzy, pressing on the floor with her feet to raise her backside from the bench, offering her sex to him in the most lewd and wanton manner, caring only for the roughness of the knife handle.

He had forced it in to the hilt now, and he twisted it again, bringing a hoarse cry from her lips. He reached up and ran his hands over her stiff nipples. Her entire body was in a state of delicious tension as she strained upward. A film of sweat had broken out on her body, making her breasts glisten in the harsh light of the room.

Her mind was a whirl. She knew he shouldn't be doing this to her. She knew too that she should be fighting it, that he had no right to strip her and abuse her in this way. But the sheer eroticism of the situation overwhelmed her. She was stark naked, bound and helpless, her breasts and sex bare and unprotected, being subjected to the most intimate assault imaginable, and she was responding with a lustful passion she had not known herself capable of.

He began moving the knife handle in and out, twisting it gently as he did so, allowing the rough surface to stimulate her clitoris so that she whimpered with pleasure. It was moving easily, lubricated by her juices, sliding inside her until the cold metal of the hilt came in contact with her love bud, giving her a shock of delight then slipping back again until only the knob at its end remained inside her. Then it would begin its journey inside again, making a wet sound as it did. She was like a pagan sacrifice on an altar in some obscure religious rite, about to be run through with a sacred dagger, only she was being stabbed with the blunt end of the knife, and in the most private part of her body.

His movements became faster. An urgency seemed to have gripped him and he rammed the knife handle hard into her. She responded, thrusting her hips up at him, stretching her legs still wider so that her clitoris stood proud from her sex lips. He reached for her breasts, which were dancing deliciously to the rhythm of his thrusts. His hand closed around her firm soft globes, rubbing the nipples, damp with his saliva and her sweat.

He could see she was close to her climax. She too realised that she was about to humiliate herself by submitting to him in such an obvious and degrading manner. But her lust was too great. She was crying out with every stroke, her arse slapping up and down on the bench as she thrust her sex at the object of assault. Her body stiffened, she arched herself, her bottom clear of the bench.

He slowed his movements, trying to control her, to delay and then prolong the climax that he knew was close. He played her like some delicate instrument, bringing her to the brink with his careful manipulation, sensing her reaching her peak and then stopping so that she remained suspended on the edge, her body still arched upward in delightful tension, her breath coming in harsh bursts, her eyes shut tight.

Then, at last, she could hold it no longer and with a cry from deep in her throat she finally succumbed to her passion, the sheer animal pleasure of her orgasm washing over her as her juices flowed. Her hips thrust hard at the knife handle as she released her lust, abandoning herself completely with no thought for modesty or decorum, naked and red-faced in the watchman's seedy apartment.

He continued his thrusts, slowing them as he felt the ebbing of her fervour. The stiffness began to leave her limbs and her body sank back onto the bench, into the pool of wetness that had flowed from her. His movements became less and less, until finally he stopped, leaving the weapon embedded in its victim.

She lay back, exhausted and ashamed at her lasciviousness, her exquisite breasts rising and falling as she fought to regain her breath. She couldn't believe what had happened; that her body had betrayed her so in giving the depraved swine his pleasure. She closed her eyes, wishing the ordeal would end, that he would free her, allow her to cover herself, to hide from his gaze. But when she opened them again he was still there, and she was still harshly exposed to his gaze.

He spoke at last. "That was fun, wasn't it?"

She turned away. "Will you let me go now?" she whispered.

He grinned. "What already? But we've only just begun. I've got something much better to put in that wet little love-hole of yours."

She was suddenly angry. "You said just a workout. Well I worked out."

"You certainly did. And very entertaining it was too."

She blushed. "Listen," she said, "if you don't free me I'll scream this place down until someone comes."

"What if they do? Who's in the more compromised position? You, coming to my room in the middle of the night stark naked and having to be restrained, or me, the innocent watchman?"

"Nobody would believe that. Besides, I was wearing..."

"What? That old floor cloth over there? And even if you were, wandering into my room in the middle of the night with your arse and cunt bare is going to look pretty provocative. At best you'd lose your job, and your bed. Then where would you be?"

She was silent for a while, her mind racing. What he said was true. She had compromised herself by entering his room at night in a state of undress, and she knew she'd have difficulty proving herself entirely innocent. They'd never keep her on after such a scandal. Then an idea began to form in her mind. "What about the rat?" she asked.

"What rat?" he said.

"The one in my room. At least that will prove my story."

He considered this for a while. She could see she had shaken his confidence. She prayed he would take the bait.

"You may be right," he said at last. "I guess I'd better get rid of the rat. Meantime we'll do something to stop you making any unnecessary noises."

She watched apprehensively as he picked up a rubber ball from the table. It was about an inch and a half in diameter, the type bodybuilders squeeze to strengthen their grip. He tossed it in the air a couple of times, then leant over her.

"Open your mouth."

She shook her head, terrified.

He held his fist close to her face. "Open up, I said. That's if you want to keep your teeth."

She opened her mouth. He forced the ball between her teeth so that her mouth was jammed open. The ball was hard and tasted of rubber, and she bit down on it, trying not to panic. He produced the tape from his pocket again and holding her hair from her face, wrapped it round her mouth and behind her head, making a number of turns so that the ball was held securely in place.

"So much for screaming," he said when he had finished. "Still, better kill that rat, be on the safe side, eh?"

He winked at her, running his hands roughly over her breasts, down her body to her sex, where the knife was still embedded. He twisted it back and forth and was amused to see her writhe and moan slightly. "Plenty of time for that." He grinned. Then he picked up a large Indian club and was gone.

The moment he was out the door Lia began to move. She knew she didn't have much time, that she had to free herself before he returned. First her hands. The rings on her wristbands were looped around the weightlifting bar. If only she could reach out far enough, she would be able to free her hands.

She pulled down hard. Nothing. She tried again. This time when she relaxed there was a clank from behind her. She had moved the weights! She redoubled her efforts and was rewarded by the bar moving down half an inch. If it moved half an inch it would move further.

She dragged the bar down, drawing on reserves of strength she hadn't known she possessed. Gradually it descended, inch by painful inch until the cold metal rested on her breasts. Then she began moving her right hand, struggling to keep the bar down as her fingers crept out along the bar. Half an inch to go, then a quarter. Her chest felt as if it would burst with the strain. Her arm was almost at full stretch and it hurt terribly. Her face was going from red to purple and she knew she would have to breathe out soon. But to breathe out now would be to relax her muscles, to let go of the bar. With a final superhuman effort she stretched her arm to the limit that her muscles and sinews would allow, and suddenly the ring dropped from the end of the bar and she was free!

She let go of it, and once again the weights sprang back with a crash. She wondered vaguely if the noise would be audible from her room, but guessed not. She allowed herself a few moments regaining her breath, then she was moving again.

She slipped the other ring from the handle easily, then sat up, rubbing her sore wrists. Her legs were still fastened to the bench and she scrabbled at the tape with her fingers, trying to free them. If only she had something... she almost laughed at her own stupidity. She lay back on the bench and eased the knife handle from her vagina, careful not to cut herself on its fierce blade. It came out slowly, with a squelching sound, the knob on the end rubbing against the inside of her sex, momentarily stimulating her again. Then it was out, its handle wet and slippery in her hands.

She sat up again and set about the tape. It sliced apart easily and soon she was standing up, stretching to ease the stiffness in her limbs.

She was thinking fast. It was no good just trying to avoid him, or to run away either. For a start she was naked, her T-shirt ruined. No, she would have to put him out of action. She looked about the room for something she could use.

Piled in one corner was a series of weights, of the kind that attached to a barbell. She examined them. They were very heavy. She looked at the door. He had left it slightly ajar, and that gave her a chance.

She dragged the chair she had earlier been sitting on across to the door. Then she went to the weights. She gripped one and lifted. It was heavy. Very heavy. She staggered across the room with it, all the time listening for his footfall. Her jaw ached with the gag, but she daren't take it out just yet.

She climbed onto the chair with difficulty, clutching the weight. Then with a deep breath she heaved it above her head and onto the top of the door. She rested for a moment, then adjusted it so that it bridged the gap between the top of the door and the frame.

She briefly admired her handiwork. Then she climbed down from the chair, replacing it where she had found it and returned to the bench.

In order for the plan to work he had to suspect nothing. That meant he would have to find her as he had left her. Though she longed to cover herself from his lustful gaze she would have to endure her exposure for a little longer. She sat astride the bench. She had been careful to cut the tape around her ankles at the back, and had left the tape itself still stuck to her leg so it was just a matter of placing her ankles where they had been secured. Similarly she guessed he would not immediately notice that her hands were no longer attached. There was still the matter of the knife though.

She sat astride the bench again, then lying back, took the weapon and began easing it back into her vagina. Slowly, twisting it slightly as he had, she pressed it into herself, the feel of its cold roughness in her vagina making her catch her breath. Further it went, until she felt filled by it. She felt a pang of shame to think she was deliberately going to expose herself like that, her naked breasts on display, her sex filled with the ugly weapon.

She had no time to contemplate her predicament, however. Outside she heard a footfall in the hallway. She lay back at once, grasping the handles and spreading her legs, holding them tightly against the bench supports. She watched the door apprehensively.

A hand came through the gap. It was holding something. She fought back the nausea as she recognised the rat, hanging by its tail, its head smashed and bloody. The hand shook it up and down, causing blood to drip onto the floor. Then a head came round the door. He was grinning. "Surprise!" he said, his eyes wandering up and down her body.

Lia froze. What if he looked up? He would see the weight and her plan would be ruined. Worse, he would be very angry. She considered for a moment whether she would be able to get the knife out of her vagina in time to fight him off. Then he moved.

"Time to fuck, Number Seventeen..." he shoved open the door.

The edge of the weight slipped from the top of the door and toppled downwards. It struck him just above the left temple with a sickening thud. He stood staring stupidly at her and for a terrible moment she thought she had failed. Then his eyes glazed over and he toppled forward like a felled tree, catching his forehead a second blow on the corner of the chest of drawers as he went down. He hit the floor and lay still.

Lia sat up fearfully. He wasn't moving. She got to her feet and crouched down to examine him. He had gone a strange shade of blue, and blood was seeping from both of the wounds on his head. She tried to find a pulse, fumbling clumsily with his wrist. She could find nothing. Oh God, she'd killed him!

Panic engulfed her. Fingerprints! She would be tried for murder. She gazed wildly about. She would need the key to the main door. She sat back on the bench and gently extracted the knife for the second time. It slid from her easily. She held it for a moment, running her fingers over its rough curved surface, recalling the delicious sensations it had invoked. Then she put it aside. She had to escape.

A brief search of the top drawer of the chest revealed the watchman's set of keys. Beside it in the drawer was a pile of banknotes. She could use some money if she was going to be on the run. She glanced at the prone body. After all, she thought, she had earned it. May as well get hung for a sheep as a lamb. She closed her fist about the money and the keys and made for the door. She took a final look around, then switching out the light the naked girl headed for her room, hoping desperately that no one would be about.

Within thirty minutes, a bundle of her belongings slung over her shoulder, she unlocked the hostel door and was heading for the city gate.

Chapter 2

The Highway

All that had been two weeks ago now, and to Lia it just seemed like a bad dream. The two weeks had been spent travelling, often walking for whole days, snatching meals where she could and trying to stay inconspicuous.

Once outside the city, away from the city police forces, she was much less afraid of the consequence of her crime. The forces were in general divided from city to city and seldom passed on more than rudimentary details of fugitives unless their crime was particularly heinous. Outside the city the Defence Force was in charge, a paramilitary organisation that spent much of its time policing the highways.

The countryside, therefore, was still an unsafe environment, though for a girl like Lia, brought up in the harsh city, it seemed quiet and inviting. As she stood in the shallows of the river, soaping her breasts and feeling the sunshine on her bare back, it seemed like a paradise.

She rinsed the suds from her and watched as the current carried them downstream. She stood for a while, enjoying the feel of the water as it flowed past, her eyes closed, face upturned to the blue sky, looking like a young Venus emerging from the deep. She felt free and happy in this moment. She just wanted to drift along with the water. And what was stopping her? She tossed the bar of soap onto the bank and crouching down, let herself float onto her back. Paddling gently with her feet, only her face and breasts visible above the water, she drifted gently with the river.

The coolness of it, the warmth of the sun on her face, the sheer peace of the moment sent her briefly into a dreamlike state as she shut her troubles from her mind, drifting lazily with the flow.

Suddenly she felt the current begin to tug harder at her. She opened her eyes and gazed about. In her inattention she had drifted out into the middle of the river where the flow of water was much stronger. The bank where her clothes and belongings lay was fast receding as she was washed downriver.

She struck out strongly for the bank, stroking and kicking hard against the current, flailing her arms and legs in a desperate attempt to get back to her things. But the current continued to carry her away. The small bundle of belongings was no more than a speck now and as the current carried her round a bend in the river it was lost from view.

The high, inaccessible banks whisked past her as she rushed on. She gazed up at the trees overhanging the river as they drifted overhead. On either side the wood continued, dense as ever. She was feeling cold now, the cool water chilled by the fast flow. She felt her limbs begin to stiffen and knew she would have to escape soon.

Far ahead the river took a sweeping turn to the right and she could just make out a spot on the left-hand shore where the banks seemed lower. As she approached she discerned a fallen tree that stretched out into the current. She watched it carefully as it came closer. It was a large old tree, still retaining many of its branches, and it looked sturdy enough to take her weight easily.

Closer and closer it came, and harder and harder she swam, her eyes fixed on her target. She had reached the bend of the river and the pull against her was becoming even stronger. Still she struggled on, her arms and legs aching with the effort. The tree was only ten yards away, its branches tantalisingly close. Desperately she flung her arms in its direction and her hands closed about a branch. It was thin and slippery with the slime of the river, but she clung on, and all at once was still and felt the full force of the current dragging her, trying to snatch her back into its flow.

With a great effort she began hauling herself through the branches, climbing ever higher until at last she was clear of the water. Then she walked carefully up the length of the trunk, arms outstretched, grabbing at a suitable branch where she could find one.

She reached the base, crouched down and dropped nimbly from the tree onto the soft grass, where she lay, panting with the shock as much as the exertion. It had been a close thing. She doubted she could have lasted much longer in the water. The cold and her exhaustion had been almost too much. She closed her eyes and tried not to think about it.

As she lay there, her mind becoming clearer, she suddenly realised she was no longer wearing the loincloth. The tow of the current must have pulled it from her while she was clinging to the tree. She gave a gasp of dismay as she realised she was completely naked, with nothing she could use to cover herself.

For a while she stood uncertain what to do. She wanted desperately to find her clothes. She estimated the river must have carried her at least three miles. There was nothing else for it. She had to try to make her way back. It was the only plan she had.

She set out through the forest, picking her route carefully between the trees and bushes. She planned to follow the course of the river upstream, but soon realised this was easier said than done. Thick outcrops of bushes grew right to the water's edge, making passing impossible, so she was forced to penetrate deeper into the wood, diverting around large expanses of stinging nettles and thistles, all the time drifting further from the river. Soon she was completely disoriented. Continual backtracking and change of direction had confused her utterly in the closeness of the wood. One tree looked just like another, one clearing like the one she had just left. There was nothing by which to navigate, no landmarks to take a bearing by.

Then she had an idea. If she could climb one of the taller trees perhaps she would be able to get a better idea of the lie of the land, at least give herself some sense of direction. It was worth a try. She looked about and chose a tall specimen, the branches of which hung low so she could climb quite easily.

She started upwards, careful not to scratch her unprotected skin on the rough bark. The branches were set at just the right distance apart, making the climb relatively simple. She was soon some distance from the floor of the forest, climbing swiftly. To anyone passing, the view of the girl from below would have afforded a delightful vision, the perfect globes of her arse stretched taut as she climbed, her pink sex inviting, making her appear for all the world like some naked wood nymph escaping the clutches of a lusty satyr.

As she climbed higher the trunk of the tree thinned and the branches became less substantial. She stepped carefully up from one branch to another, clinging on tightly. One more branch, then at last she was clear of the treetops around her, out of the darkness of the forest. She squinted into the bright sunlight.

She was about sixty feet above the ground, clinging precariously to the swaying tree. Below her lay a wide forested valley, the treetops stretching to the horizon. Nothing but trees for mile after mile, a great swathe of green as far as she could see. Her heart sank at the sight of such a featureless horizon. Then she noticed that the landscape wasn't as completely empty as she first thought. At intervals of about a mile she could just make out straight dark lines that ran between the trees, each parallel to the other. They were fire breaks. Wide swathes cut through the forest to prevent the spread of fires. Never having seen a large forest before, Lia had no idea of their purpose, but she recognised them as a way of navigating through the dense undergrowth, of at least giving her a sense of direction as she walked.

Then a sudden flash caught her eye as something reflected the sunlight far below. She gazed intently in the direction from which it had come. Something was moving about a mile and a half from where she hung in the tree. She continued watching and was rewarded by another flash. Then she began to make out a shape, moving at some speed, then she heard the unmistakable sound of the air horn of a truck, echoing eerily from the sides of the valley. It was a highway, and that meant people!

Without further ado she began climbing down, swinging agilely through the branches with a newfound energy, dropping from branch to branch in her anxiety to be on her way towards the highway.

Once down she set out resolutely for the fire break. She had been careful to gauge the sun's direction whilst up the tree, so she was confident of finding her way.

Even so, it took her longer than she had anticipated. On two or three occasions she came across vast expanses of nettles, growing waist high. They would have been daunting enough to a clothed person, but naked they were out of the question and necessitated long detours. Then at last she saw a patch of sunlight ahead, much brighter than any she had encountered up to then. She quickened her pace, stepping nimbly across fallen trees, squeezing carefully between trunks, the brightness getting closer until at last she broke cover from the woods and found herself in the broad corridor of a fire break.

Lia almost laughed with relief at getting out of the claustrophobic forest, at seeing clear blue sky above her and uninterrupted grass beneath her feet. She gazed about at the fire break. It was about fifty yards wide, with a rough track running down the centre. On either side of the track was a treeless expanse, punctuated only by a few small bushes. The gap in the trees stretched away from her on either side as far as she could see, running straight as a ruler through the woods. She picked her way through the grass. It was longer and coarser than she had at first thought and she had to take care not to scratch her bare legs as she made her way to the path.

Standing on the path, with clear space on either side of her and the cloudless sky above, Lia felt suddenly very exposed. Somehow the density of the wood had protected her. Now, out in the open, she felt her nakedness more intensely and found herself gazing round to see if there was anyone about. She laughed silently at the irony of her predicament. On the one hand she feared the idea of being seen completely nude and unprotected, and on the other she knew her salvation lay in finding other people as soon as she could.

She set off down the path in the direction of the road. The sun was warm on her face and breasts and a cool breeze blew through the trees. In a strange way it felt good to be so free and she began once again to feel at one with the countryside. Rabbits feeding by the track watched unconcerned as she passed. Every now and again a pheasant would rise up from the grass with a great clacking of wings as it tried to gain height. And Lia strode on through the middle of it, her feet leaving small footprints in the dust.

But as she came closer to the road Lia's apprehension began to return. Finding a highway was one thing, but what to do when she reached it was quite another. She was without money or clothes. What could she offer in return for something to cover her and some way to get back to civilisation?

Perhaps she could make some clothes out of the leaves. But what would she use to sew them together? Perhaps she could steal some money. But from where? And how could she use it without first finding some clothes?

In her heart Lia knew the answer, but it was some time before she would allow herself to consider it. The only bargaining counter she possessed was her body. That was what she would have to offer. To give herself to a man in exchange for money and clothing. After all she was naked, and beautiful. She would have to take advantage of the only things in her favour.

Now she had finally admitted her plan to herself, she found herself considering the prospect and was surprised to feel a strange warmth rising within her. The idea of approaching a stranger naked and offering herself to him was one she found oddly exciting. She had always secretly enjoyed showing off her body, wearing brief or see-through garments and revelling in the attention they brought. At work she would sometimes glance through the soft porn magazines her boss kept in the bottom drawer of his desk, studying the photos of the nude girls and wishing she too could display herself thus, revelling at the thought of all those male eyes upon her, of flaunting her breasts and sex in front of the camera. Now here she was, not just a photo, but alive and warm. The heat in her belly increased as she stepped out towards the highway.

The fire break ended in a low wooden fence that seemed to run the length of the forest. As she approached it, Lia's nerve began to fail again and she left the track, preferring for the time being to retain the cover of the forest. She concealed herself in the trees on the right-hand side of the break and peered over the fence at the highway.

The road ran straight in both directions from where she stood. It was wide, three lanes in each direction, a testimony to the days when such routes would have been busy with vehicles. Now it was empty. As she had been getting closer to it she monitored the passage of traffic. She estimated that trucks were passing at intervals of about two minutes. Sure enough, the growl of a large engine reached her ears almost at once and a vehicle appeared in the distance. She watched as it roared down the road and swept past the spot where she was hiding. The road ran by about forty yards from the fence, so she felt reasonably sure she would not be seen, at least until she wanted to be.

Lia stood for some time in the trees. For the moment her resolve had deserted her. The prospect of leaving the cover and allowing herself to be seen was almost too daunting. She ran through the options in her mind for the hundredth time, and for the hundredth time reached the same conclusion. There was no choice. Her only salvation lay in the cab of one of the trucks. A second one passed, and still she lingered, then a third. She knew she would have to move soon. It was simply a case of plucking up the courage.

Doubts began to assail her. Would they want her? Would they find her desirable? She looked down at her body. Her breasts were firm and inviting, the nipples jutting proudly. She began to stroke them, enjoying her own caresses. They hardened under her touch, so that they stood out even more invitingly. She continued to tease them, rolling them between finger and thumb and watching them swell.

Her left hand moved down to her belly. She ran it across her mound and down into the cleft beneath, stroking between the outer lips of her sex. She slid a finger inside, surprised to find herself so wet. The stroking was beginning to turn her on, and that in turn was emboldening her for what she knew she had to do. Perhaps that was the answer; to stimulate herself while she awaited the next truck. Perhaps that would signal her intentions to the driver of the vehicle. She pictured herself standing in the road, caressing her body intimately as a truck approached, and a surge of wanton lust swept through her, making her moan with desire. That was what she would do!

She looked out at the highway, still gently masturbating, holding her passion under control for the time being. As she watched another truck appeared over the brow and thundered down towards her. After this one, she promised herself. Then it would be time.

The truck roared by and on up the highway. Taking a final glance around Lia made her move.

She climbed over the low fence. Once on the other side there was no cover at all, just the open highway. She began to walk towards it. It seemed a greater distance to the roadside than she had at first thought and she began to feel very vulnerable as each step took her further and further from the safety of the trees. She was halfway across the grassy strip that divided forest and road, listening intently for the sound of an approaching vehicle.

At last she reached the edge of the highway. The road felt hot under her feet as she stepped onto its hard surface. She turned and looked back. The fence and the wood seemed a long way from her and the feeling of exposure was intense.

Her hand went back to her sex. She opened her legs and began the soft caresses once again. Her love bud was swelling and the warmth began to return. Her other hand reached for her breasts, kneading and teasing them, once more awakening a response in her nipples. She thought of what was to come, of the rough sex with a stranger in the cab of a lorry. Perhaps there would be two of them. She wondered if she could handle two. The image of two cocks inside her made her even hotter and her fingers worked at her sex with a new vigour. She wondered if they would both take her together, one in her vagina and one in her mouth. Or perhaps doggy-style, bent over the cab seats.

She was moaning softly as the images filled her head. The passion was rising in her and she felt the wetness escape from between her fingers as she moved them in and out of her vagina. Her eyes closed as the pictures in her head became more erotic. She saw herself spread-eagled on the grass verge while the two truck drivers rammed their cocks into her. Behind them she imagined others, waiting their turn.

All at once her thoughts were dragged rudely back to reality as, far in the distance, she heard the sound of a powerful motor. She opened her eyes and gazed down the road in the direction of the sound. She could see nothing as yet, but could hear the vehicle coming closer. Still she continued to caress her breasts and sex, the noise from the approaching truck a new stimulus to her passion.

Suddenly it appeared over the brow, its exhaust smoking, its engine roaring as it came in sight of the beautiful naked girl who stood on the road, legs apart, knees bent, masturbating hard.

For a moment Lia was afraid the truck would not stop as it bore down upon her at speed. She turned to face it, the exhibitionist in her rampant as she flaunted her bare body to it. Then the engine note changed and she knew it was slowing. She wished she could stop caressing herself, but somehow she seemed to be losing control.

The truck was slowing right down, coming closer and closer. She watched as it bore down upon her, its brakes squealing as it slowed. At last it came to a halt just in front of her, so close she could clearly see her body reflected in its chrome grille.

She looked up and through the windscreen. There were two men inside, rough unshaven men in red checked shirts that hung open revealing the hairs on their chests, staring at her and laughing. She glanced again at the reflection in the grille, seeing what they saw; a slim, dark-haired naked girl, legs apart, shoulders hunched, thrusting fingers urgently into her sex, her bare breasts bouncing with the rhythm of the strokes.

Suddenly Lia's courage deserted her. It had been easier when it was simply a truck she was exposing herself to. Somehow the blind windscreen and gleaming chrome had seemed less than real. Now she was gazing into the faces of the two men it all seemed somehow much more intimate. For a second she contemplated sprinting back to the woods, trying again to find her clothes, but the die was cast now. She must go on with the plan.

She slowed her masturbating, blushing red at the sight she must be making beside a public highway, but aware that her display would be having the desired effect on her potential saviours. Besides, by now she was too aroused by the eyes upon her to stop altogether.

She looked up at the two grinning men. Their gazes were fixed on her body, making her renew her efforts. She knew she should cover herself with her hands, hide her most private parts that were so publicly on display, but a reckless wantonness possessed her.

The man in the passenger seat beckoned. Taking a deep breath she walked awkwardly round to the door of the cab, fingers still embedded in her throbbing vagina. She stopped by the side of the vehicle, waiting as he wound the window down a fraction.

"What's up, baby?"

"I need a ride." Her voice was unsteady as she panted with her exertions.

"Where's your stuff?"

"I lost it."

"What all of it?"

"Yes."

The man turned to his companion and they spoke briefly. She stood, feeling very conspicuous as she waited, still caressing her swollen clitoris. Her breathing was coming in short bursts, involuntary "ahhs" escaping as she exhaled. She hoped no more traffic would come along.

The man turned to her again. "You sure this ain't a trap?"

It was a reasonable question. Truck hijacks were not unknown, despite the efforts of the Bikers. The Bikers were a second force in the countryside. Making their own laws and living their own way they were largely outside the mainstream of life. In the early days the Defence Force had tried to curb their powers, to keep them under control, but the problem proved too great and now the two simply tolerated one another.

The Bikers, as their name suggested, rode motorcycles. Powerful gleaming machines that roared up and down the highways in packs, weaving between the lanes, skidding and sliding, leaving their signatures in the form of wide black tyre marks wherever they went. They made their living by a combination of mechanical expertise and extortion. All along the highways were the Bikers' great maintenance stations where the trucks were repaired and serviced. Once a haulage boss took out a contract with the Bikers he would know his trucks were safe from hijack, and that he could have a broken down vehicle towed in and repaired anywhere on the highway network. He paid a very high premium for this assurance, but the Bikers were careful to make it worth his while. The few firms that tried to operate independently of them suffered mysterious breakdowns, loss of their loads, their drivers beaten up and their bosses found with their throats cut.

The Bikers lived in communes around the service centres and supervised the work. Most of the heavy work was done by forced labour. Young homeless men, picked up from the streets and kept as unpaid workers. Women too would occasionally be taken, generally for domestic work in the service areas, preparing meals and coffee for the stranded drivers or manning the fuel pumps. Once taken by the Bikers few ever escaped back into normal society, though some occasionally were allowed to 'retire' after years of service, and one or two actually became Bikers themselves.

"I'm alone," she gasped. "Just look about."

The two conferred again. Lia was feeling very vulnerable and wished they would come to a decision, and at least allow her to climb up into the relative privacy of the cab.

The man addressed her again. "You know we're not supposed to take passengers."

"Please?"

"What are you offering in return?"

She hesitated, then ceasing her exertions briefly she spread her arms apart. "This," she said quietly.

The man grinned. "What can we do with it?"

"Whatever you want."

He reached for the door handle, but suddenly the grin froze on his face and he stared into the middle distance. He swore, then the engine of the truck roared and it began to move. She leapt aside as the vehicle gathered speed, leaving her standing alone and confused.

Then Lia became aware of a new sound. A deeper, throatier growl than that of the truck. She swung round and shaded her eyes. Then she saw them. Roaring down the highway, in the opposite direction to the truck, was a group of motorcycles. As they approached at high speed they weaved from one lane to another, crossing and re-crossing the central reservation at high speed, barely missing one another as they did so.

Bikers!

Lia's heart pounded. There were five of them and they were approaching her fast. No wonder the truckers had set off in such a hurry; they certainly didn't want to make themselves conspicuous to these renegades. And now Lia was facing them alone. Even as she watched she saw one of the Bikers shout to the others and point in her direction. Then they were across the road and bearing down on her.

For a split second she stood rooted to the spot, then she turned and began running blindly down the road. She should have made for the fence and the wood, but in her panic she simply ran away from them.

In a matter of seconds they were up with her. She veered to one side, but found one of them alongside her, driving her back towards the rest like a cowboy rounding up a maverick heifer. She ran on in desperation, but knew it was hopeless. Her tired legs were no match for the speed and manoeuvrability of their steeds. She finally came to a halt at the roadside, exhausted with the effort of running. They drove the cycles round her in a circle, hemming her in, then stopped and kicked down their stands. She stood in the centre, her hands across her breasts and sex in a vain attempt to cover her nakedness.

One of the Bikers dismounted. "Well, well," he grinned. "What have we here?"

Lia said nothing, her eyes downcast.

He grasped her by the chin, forcing her head up so that their eyes met. "What are you doing here?" he asked, menacing.

Lia swallowed hard, trying to find her voice. "I... I was lost," she said timidly.

"Looks like that's not the only thing that's lost," he replied, to laughter from the others. "Is that why the truck was stopped?"

"I wanted a ride."

"You look to me as if you were the one giving the ride."

More laughter. "What are you doing wandering about the roads like that? Not that we're complaining, are we lads?"

It was clear that they weren't; their gazes were avid, somehow stimulating.

"What about showing a bit more?" said another.

"Yeah," said the first. "What about giving us a better look?"

"Yeah. Move those hands. Give us a good look."

The first man moved towards her and she backed away. Suddenly she felt herself grabbed from behind. A pair of strong hands gripped her elbows, forcing them behind her back. Something cold touched her skin.

Snap! Snap! Someone had produced handcuffs and closed them on her wrists, trapping her arms behind her back. No longer able to cover herself she stood exposed to the unruly mob.

The first Biker stood back and eyed her up and down. "Very nice," he said. He reached out towards her breasts. She shrank backwards. "Stand still."

Lia reacted to the order instinctively, freezing. His hand caressed her breasts, squeezing them gently, feeling the nipples as they hardened under his touch. He reached out his other hand so that both breasts were cupped in his grip. He lifted, as if weighing them, and as he did so the nipples became even more prominent.

"Nice!" he said. She remained silent, the eyes of the Bikers upon her. "Open your legs." Once again the voice carried an authority she found hard to disobey. She moved her legs apart, aware that attention had shifted to her exposed sex. "Wider."

"No!" The word escaped involuntarily from her lips. A truck was passing on the highway and she was conscious of its occupants' eyes upon her as she stood in the ring of motorcycles.

"What did you say?"

"I... you have no right."

"No right? You are walking along our highway, stark naked, trying to persuade some truck driver to fuck you, and you accuse us of having no right? I think you deserve a lesson, you frigging whore. Now open up your legs and let's see what you were so willing to offer to a couple of highway bums five minutes ago."

Lia hung her head, cowed by this verbal onslaught. She spread her legs.

"Now bend your knees and give us a decent view."

Lia was unable to explain what happened next. She knew she was trapped, that they had her in their power. She knew there was no escape, but some desperate streak in her reacted to his demand. Summoning all her strength she brought her knee up hard into his groin, causing him to double up in pain. At once she was running, headed for the fence and the cover of the forest in a last desperate attempt to escape.

She got no more than a few yards before she felt her arm grabbed from behind, yanking her fiercely round. A hand struck her across the face and as quickly as it had flared the fight went out of her. Head hanging, she allowed herself to be led back to the circle of bikes, where the man was still nursing his crotch.

"Bring her here!" he barked. She was dragged across to where he was standing. He grabbed her by the hair, forcing her head back. "I think it's time to thrash some of the insolence out of this little bitch," he said. "Get the cuffs."

He strode out across the open highway, dragging her by the hair. She scuttled behind him, struggling to keep her balance as he yanked her along. She tried to see where they were going. At the side of the road stood a sign, supported by two metal posts about five feet apart. The weather-beaten signboard, which she was unable to read since they were behind it, spanned between the posts about seven feet up.

When they reached it the brute released her, and she stood silent, her heart racing. She felt her arms grabbed from behind. There was a click and her hands were free. She brought them round in front of her, the cuffs still attached to her right arm, and rubbed her wrists.

"OK, Zep." The one she had kicked addressed one of the band, a heavy man with a large beer gut and shaggy beard. "Shackle her."

Lia watched in alarm as beer gut approached her. He took hold of her arm, the one still cuffed. Stretching it up above her head he attached the other end round a bolt that secured the sign to the post, so she was trapped, her arm above her head. Then he grabbed her other arm and snapped on a second pair of cuffs. He stretched that arm upwards too, fitting the cuff to the bolt on the opposite side. Having incapacitated her hands he proceeded to attach manacles to her legs, pulling them brutally apart and securing them to the poles.

Lia was spread-eagled at full stretch, her arms and legs wide apart, her breasts tight under the tension from the cuffs, her sex open and unprotected, her backside presented for punishment, completely at the mercy of her captors.

Zep turned to the first one, who she now recognised as their leader. "OK, Perce," he said. "She's all yours."

He approached her and reached out a hand, running it through her hair. His hand dropped to the smooth skin of her shoulders, then down to her breasts, cupping them and gently caressing the nipples. Then he reached for her sex, his fingers slipping easily into her vagina. It was still wet with the stimulation she had been giving it so publicly only a few minutes before, and he whistled quietly.

He showed his wet fingers to his companions. "Little bitch is turned on!"

His hand went to his belt, and she watched anxiously as he undid the buckle, sliding it out of the loops of his tattered jeans. He doubled the belt over, holding the ends in his right hand and slapping the loop against his open palm.

"Now," he said, "you're going to learn a lesson in manners." Then before Lia realised what was happening he raised the belt and brought it cracking down on her backside.

Thwack! The leather struck her hard, catching her left buttock. She gave a cry of surprise and pain, as much shocked as hurt by the blow.

"There!" he said. "You're going to have to learn to behave yourself, bitch."

The men wandered back to their bikes, leaving her hanging where she was. The leader reached into a bag that hung from the back of his machine and pulled out a six-pack, tossing a can to each of his companions. Lia licked her lips. She would have liked that sixth can. She watched him replace it in the bag.

The men sat down on the seats of their machines and pulled the tabs from the cans, swigging the beer and belching noisily. As they drank an animated discussion ensued. Lia strained to hear what they were saying. She managed to pick up snatches, despite the distance and the roar of the occasional truck, its occupants slowing to ogle the captive girl.

The leader was speaking. "We're not even searching for workers; it's not as if we need another girl."

"Yeah, let's face it, it's men we're short of."

"But just look at that lovely arse. It seems a shame to waste it."

"But what are we going to do with her?"

"I know what I'd do with her!"

"What?"

Thankfully the reply was drowned by the sound of a truck moving up the road, its occupants craning round for a better look at the naked girl.

"...After all, there's always the auction."

The truck had passed and she was again able to hear them.

"That's a point. We can easily fake an indenture, and she'd raise a good price. Especially as she is now."

"She'd certainly be an attraction."

"Yeah, that's settled then. We're taking her. After all, you don't get an opportunity like this every day."

"And those tits..."

The men laughed, pouring the dregs of beer down their throats and tossing the cans aside. They stood up and the one called Zep crossed to where Lia hung. He pulled a bunch of keys from his pocket and released her. She stood stiffly, rubbing her sore wrists, feeling the circulation return to her hands. She spoke quietly, not meeting his eyes. "Could I have a drink, please?"

He called across to the leader. "She wants a drink."

The man reached into his bag and pulled out the remaining can. He threw it across to her and she caught it deftly, remembering the last time a can had been thrown for her. She pulled the tab and drank thirstily, draining it. The beer tasted good, cooling her. She wiped her mouth on her forearm and tossed the empty tin away.

Zep took her hands and fastened them behind her back again, then led her across to the circle of bikes. He indicated the leader's machine. "Get on." he ordered.

Lia sat gingerly on the seat, her bottom still red with the beating she had received. She felt the man take her ankles and fasten them to shackles attached beside the footrests. Then he dragged her hands back and she felt him fit the cuffs to a ring behind the seat. She was shackled for the journey.

The leader stood over her, almost absentmindedly running a hand over her breast. "Ever ride a bike?"

She shook her head.

"Just sit still, and lean the way I do."

He mounted the machine and kicked the engine into life. The bike roared and the vibration of the powerful motor between her legs was somehow sensuous. The others had started too, and with a wave of his hand he let in his clutch and the small convoy, with its conspicuous passenger, set off up the road.

Lia had a little time to think as they sped along. So she was be in the service of these men, at least until this auction they had mentioned. To obey their every whim. To suffer their humiliations and punishments. Now that the decision had been made she felt strangely calm. She'd had a tough life to date. Nothing they could throw at her, be it the thrashings, the humiliations, the duties they would make her perform, nothing could be worse than the squalid orphanages, the cruel schools or the drudging work of her life so far. She sat as erect as she was able in her bondage, staring round at her new masters, trying not to show fear as they carried her off to her fate.

Chapter 3
The Diner

The Bikers rode on for some while, the steady drone of the engines on the long straight highway dulling the girl's senses so that she dozed, resting her head against the back of the man in front of her. She lost all sense of time and distance as the countryside flashed past. Occasionally one of the other riders would pull alongside and a shouted conversation would take place, but apart from that the journey was without incident.

Then something roused her and she lifted her head and looked about. The bikes were slowing down. She craned up and peered over the rider's shoulder. They were approaching a diner; she could see the neon signs and the great wire fence that surrounded it. As she watched they pulled off the highway and came to a halt at the gates. The man produced a card from his pocket and swiped it through a reading device mounted on a pole beside the road. The gates swung open and the Bikers roared in, the gate swinging shut behind them.

The diner was like a hundred others lining the expressways that crisscrossed the country. Outside the dilapidated neon signs flashed their message of the delights to be had within. Beer. Coke. Burgers. All the junk food, booze and grease you could manage.

The parking lot was full of the great armoured trucks that were virtually the sole form of traffic on the roads these days. Encased in bulletproof cocoons the drivers would haul their loads from city to city in these monsters, a radio line to the nearest Defence Force team their only lifeline in the event of a breakdown. These diners were the sole oases on their long and solitary journeys, and all were equipped with the coded magnetic cards that proclaimed their legitimacy and allowed them to enter the gates that surrounded the building, making it a virtual fortress. How the Bikers had come by a card Lia could only guess.

They sped across the parking lot, swinging left and drawing up in line across the entrance. The five of them dismounted, leaving Lia still chained to the machine.

The name above the door, Pete's Place, caught her eye. She had stopped there about a week before, entering by the heavily protected pedestrian entrance at the back. Her heart sank as she recalled the details of her previous visit.

She had sat at the bar and ordered a beer from a bored looking barmaid who ignored her. She'd had to order a second and third time before the girl wandered nonchalantly across the bar and thrust a beer and a dirty glass in front of her. Lia drank the liquor quickly and left without tipping, though she knew the barmaid's living would depend on tips.

"Bitch," the girl had called after her.

"Bitch yourself," she spat back, slamming the door behind her.

Back then she thought she'd seen the last of the place and its arrogant young employee. Now she found herself back, and in very different circumstances. She hoped fervently she would not be taken inside, or that the girl would not be there. At least, she thought, they must allow her to cover up. No one could be expected to enter such a place in her present state. Perhaps they would give her a coat, or at least leave her outside cuffed to the bikes. She couldn't bear the thought of entering the diner again.

The leader of the group, the one called Perce, spoke to her. "Wanna eat?"

She shook her head, gazing down at the ground.

He grabbed her by the chin, pulling her face to his. "Answer me. Wanna eat?"

She tried to speak, but words refused to come. He stepped back, then suddenly slapped her, so that she let out a sharp cry.

"So, you can speak after all. What about it?"

"Not in there," she muttered.

"Well you'll just have to come in and watch us," he said.

He reached down and undid the locks holding her ankles bound to the bike, then released the cuffs from the ring on the seat, leaving her hands still fastened behind her.

Lia felt panic rising in her. "But you can't make me go in there like this!"

He smiled. "Like what?"

She lowered her eyes again. "You know."

He grinned, his eyes piercing hers. "You tell me," he said.

She hesitated. "I'm naked," she said quietly, blushing at having to make the admission.

"What?" he said, pretending to cup his ear.

Lia's face reddened more deeply. "I'm naked," she repeated, this time a little louder.

"I'm sorry," he grinned, "I just can't seem to hear you. Maybe it's the noise of the traffic. Perhaps you'd better tell me once we're inside, and in a nice loud voice or I'll have to take my belt to you again."

By now Zep and the others had gone ahead of them, and stood waiting by the open door. Perce shoved her from behind and she found herself inside.

The diner was as she remembered it. Plastic-topped tables, each with salt pepper and sauce, fluorescent lighting that cast a flat glare over the whole place. At the far end a bar with half empty liquor bottles lining the shelf behind it. The floor was covered with linoleum, dirty and faded and scarred with the burn marks of a thousand cigarette butts.

The room was about half full. At the tables sat men in dirty overalls, smoking and picking at grease-covered plates. In one corner sat another group of Bikers, drinking beer and laughing noisily. Through a hatch in the wall a fat man in a dirty vest was stacking plates and behind the bar sat that same barmaid, absently filing her nails. At one or two of the tables men nudged one another and pointed to Lia, grinning. In vain she searched the faces for one that offered solace from her plight.

Perce nudged her in the ribs. "Now what was it you were trying to tell me? Nice and loud now." His hand reached menacingly for his belt.

She gazed at him pleadingly. "Please?" she whispered. He began to undo his belt. Lia took a deep breath. Just in front of her, on a pillar, was a full-length mirror, placed there in better days to allow the clients to adjust their clothing before leaving. It reflected her body, and she studied it momentarily.

She saw a slim, willowy figure, dark hair draped across her shoulders, breasts not overlarge, firm and jutting proudly, the dark nipples prominent and upturned, her belly dark with downy pubic hair kept trimmed so that the lips of her sex were clearly visible, her long shapely legs tapering gracefully. She was probably the most beautiful woman these louts would ever see clothed, let alone as she was. And she took heart from that.

"I'm naked," she said in a loud clear voice.

The talking died, and all eyes turned in her direction. She watched their reactions anxiously, her eyes moving from face to face, trying to stare them down when their eyes met. Some grinned, others chuckled and whispered to their companions. One or two just sat open-mouthed.

Her brief moment of courage deserted her and the full enormity of her vulnerability sank home. Not only were her charms openly on display, but with her hands fastened behind her she had no possible way of covering herself. Any hopes she had entertained of mercy or rescue were dashed. Clearly the power of the Bikers was such that if she was in their hands no one was about to challenge them. Her eyes stopped scanning the faces of the audience, looking away and her head dropped as she awaited her captors' next order.

Suddenly she looked up again. An eye had caught hers, its expression somehow different from the rest. The man sat with the other group of Bikers. Like them he was clad in leather, his jacket open to the waist revealing a mass of blond curls on his chest. His eyes were deep blue and compassionate. His face was somehow kind, framed in long blond tresses of hair that hung to his shoulders. To Lia he appeared like the prince she had always imagined in the fairy-tales she'd read as a child. She continued to stare at him, transfixed by his gaze.

For what seemed an age no one spoke, then Perce made a beckoning gesture and Lia awoke from her reverie as she was shoved forward. The six of them, Lia in front, crossed the room, she still unable to take her eyes off the man at the table.

"Here," Perce barked, indicating a table with five seats by the wall. The seats scraped back and the five sat, Lia left standing beside them, glad to be facing away from the other customers but unsure what she should do.

"Beers?" They nodded. Perce turned to her. "Turn round."

Lia hesitated, unsure what he wanted and unwilling to face the crowd again. Then she saw he had a key in his hand.

"Turn," he repeated. Slowly she obeyed, still keeping her eyes downcast. She felt him grasp her wrists and then a click signified that her hands were free at last.

She longed to cover her breasts and sex, hide them from the eyes of the crowd, but her instincts told her to leave her hands hanging at her sides. She turned again to face him.

"Five beers."

She hesitated, startled. Surely he wasn't sending her to the bar? Amongst all those men? Couldn't they wait for the barmaid?

"Wassamatter, you deaf? Five frigging beers!"

"But I'm... she paused. There was no point in repeating what was obvious to all in the room.

"I know, we all know. That's your problem. If you hadn't been flaunting your body to one and all when we found you things might be different. Now get going."

So this was to be her first test; to wait on them. In any other circumstances it would have seemed a small chore, but in this place, in her current state, it was a dreadful prospect. However she knew she dare not fail them. She was all theirs now and her job was to obey. Well, she would show them she wasn't afraid of a few men ogling her body.

Lia took a deep breath and turned back towards the bar. Head erect and eyes looking neither right nor left she crossed the room. As she passed between the tables stage-whispered comments, clearly meant for her ears, were passed between the occupants.

"Nice arse."

"Yeah, and it looks like it's been thrashed as well."

"Wouldn't mind doing that myself."

"I know what I'd like to do to her."

In front of her the men standing at the bar closed ranks slightly, obliging her to push between them. Then came the moment she dreaded. She knew she would have to address the barmaid.

She cleared her throat. "Five beers," she said, her voice sounding unnaturally loud amidst the silence that had descended over the room.

The girl continued filing her nails, apparently unaware. "Five beers," Lia repeated. The girl looked up.

"You talking to me?"

"Yeah. Five beers." Lia did her best to sound authoritative.

"You lost your manners as well as your clothes?"

Lia reddened at the remark. "Five beers, please," she muttered.

"S'better." The girl rose lazily from her stool and began opening the bottles. She put a tray on the bar and loaded it with the drinks and glasses. As she did so she gazed at Lia's face and her eyes narrowed.

"Wait a minute. Weren't you in here last week?"

Lia's heart sank. "May have been," she said, trying to sound disinterested.

"Yeah, I remember now. Uppity little bitch, weren't you? Didn't leave no tip. I'll have to have a word with your friends about that. Don't like uppity little bitches in here. Specially bare-assed ones." She reached across the bar and ran her hand over Lia's breast. "Bin slapping yer tits as well as yer arse by the look of it," she grinned. "I might just try and get them to do a little more of that." She grasped Lia's nipple between thumb and forefinger and pinched. Lia gave a little yelp of pain. The girl smirked. "Better get those drinks over pretty quick or they're liable to get cross."

Lia lifted the tray.

"Careful guys!" the barmaid called to the rest of the bar. "Lady's got her hands full!"

The remark was not lost on the drinkers. As Lia began to back away from the bar she was only too aware of the vulnerability of her breasts, jutting conspicuously over the tray of drinks, and of her naked, unprotected sex.

The men crowded in around her, hands groping. One openly caressed her right breast whilst behind her she felt a hand slide down the crack of her backside. More men pushed about her. Hands seemed to come from all sides, squeezing her nipples, caressing her buttocks. A finger ran over her pubic hair and touched her sex. She was alarmed at the excitement she felt, and a familiar wetness begin to rise in her belly as the touches became more intimate.

She found herself forced back, so that she was half sitting on the edge of one of the tables. Hands grabbed her legs, forcing them apart. One of the men sitting at the table pulled his chair so he was positioned between her legs. He ran his hand up the inside of her thigh and his fingers prised apart her sex lips, exposing her clitoris. He began to rub her love button, making it swell, and causing the wetness between her legs to increase.

Suddenly overcome by sheer physical desire she involuntarily opened her legs still further. Her mind was a confusion of overwhelming desire and shame at her lasciviousness. She felt an orgasm welling up, try as she might to fight it. The room swam round as she thrust her thighs against the caressing hands, the bottles and glasses on the tray rattling together and threatening to overturn.

More hands were upon her. She felt one from under the table grope between her thighs and penetrate her with its fingers. She cried out with pleasure as she was manipulated by a dozen hands. Careless of her nudity, of where she was, of who was doing it, she abandoned herself to her lust completely.

"Enough." The voice of Perce rang across the room. "I'm getting thirsty here."

All at once the caresses stopped, as the men obeyed his order. The one between her legs removed his fingers, making her cry out with disappointment. He held his hand aloft for all to see how wet it was. He wiped it on her belly, making shiny damp streaks down her, and matting her pubic hair.

For a while she was unable to move. Her hands shook as she struggled to keep hold of the tray. Her legs remained wide apart, even though the men had released them. Then slowly she regained her composure and the deep shame of her desires overcame her. She tried to stand, but the crowd was too close.

"Excuse me," she finally mumbled lamely.

The men grinned but remained where they were, watching to see what she would do.

"Come on guys," she pleaded, "let me through."

Then they were standing aside. For a moment she was unable to understand why, then she saw the tall blond Biker who had caught her eye earlier. He had intervened. One word was enough, and the men fell away.

He approached her, taking her elbow and helping her up. "OK?" he asked, his voice deep and resonant.

She nodded. Something about him made her feel safe. "You'll have to be more careful, going about like that."

She felt terribly embarrassed at her total nudity. She wanted to cover herself, hide her breasts from his gaze, to say I am yours alone, not for this rabble.

But he turned away and went back to his table. She looked across to where her companions were sitting, waiting for her. Then with a deep breath she went to them.

Perce reached out and, before she knew what he was doing, slid a finger into her sex. It came out sopping wet. "Horny little slut," he grunted. "Let's have those beers."

Lia placed the tray on the table, and still breathless began to serve the drinks, leaning across so her rear must be affording a great view to those watching. She wondered if the blond man was looking too. She remained bent over for slightly longer than was necessary in the hope that he was.

When she had finished setting out the bottles and glasses and pouring the beers, Perce indicated a bar stool beside the table.

"Up there where we can all get a good view," he said, and Lia perched herself as demurely as she was able, facing the wall.

"No, bitch, face the others." Perce stood over her, grasping her hands and making her tuck them under the seat, then placed her feet on the rails on either side of the stool, forcing her knees apart so her open sex was on full view. He lifted her chin and made her straighten her back so that her breasts were thrust forward, as if inviting the caresses of the crowd. A murmur of appreciation went up as they sat back to admire her exposure.

And so they remained, the men drinking their beers, laughing and joking while Lia sat staring ahead, trying to ignore their lewd remarks. As time passed the bar continued to fill, word having spread on the truckers' radios about the gorgeous little filly who was showing her all for free at Pete's

Place.

The sounds of the bar, its chatter and muzak, the clinking of glasses and the scraping of cutlery became mingled into a mush of noise in Lia's brain. She stayed as she had been placed, while the arriving truckers came and admired her before settling down and ordering. The Bikers continued to drink, letting the barmaid serve them. Across the room the blond man sat with his companions, apparently indifferent to Lia, though she longed for him to look in her direction. She found her mind drifting, a strange detachment overcoming her so that she was able to put her predicament out of her mind, and lose herself in her own thoughts.

Suddenly the talking died away and Lia sensed that something had changed. She glanced about and saw all eyes were on the window. Through its grimy panes she could just make out a white vehicle that had drawn up by the door. Then she realised why they were staring. It was a Defence Force armoured car.

Outside of the cities normal policing had long been an impossibility, due to the level of violence and lawlessness. Now the highways were policed by the Defence Force, a sort of paramilitary police who patrolled in armoured cars trying to maintain a minimum of law and order.

Lia's heart leapt. Thank God! She was saved! A lawman!

He would arrest the Bikers and set her free. She jumped to her feet, and was about to run to the door when a hand clamped onto her wrist.

"Where the hell are you going?" It was Zep.

"I'm..."

"Get back on the stool."

"But I... The Defence Force..."

"Sit down." The order came from Perce. Slowly she got back onto the stool.

The door opened and a broad figure filled the doorway. He was above six foot two, clad in khaki with a white helmet and dark glasses. At one hip was strapped an automatic pistol, at the other a lethal looking stick. Behind him stood a second man, similarly attired but smaller and clearly the first's junior.

The larger man removed his glasses and his eyes scanned the room. Lia instinctively covered her breasts and sex, intimidated by the intensity of his look. She expected that he would approach them immediately and begin questioning the Bikers, but instead, having taken in the scene, he strolled slowly across to the bar and exchanged a few words with the barmaid. Lia was dumbfounded. Surely he had noticed her? Surely he realised her predicament? Even if he was not going to arrest the Bikers, wouldn't he at least take her in for indecent exposure or something?

The officer finished his conversation and began moving among the tables, stopping every now and again to speak to someone, check their licence and ID card, rummage in a bag or search pockets. All the time his deputy stood beside him, watching.

At last he made his way across to the table where the Bikers were sitting.

He paused in front of Lia and slowly looked her up and down. She found herself unable to look him in the eyes and stared down, her hands still defensively trying to hide her nakedness.

He turned away and began talking to Perce in a low voice. Surely now he would release her. But the talking continued, punctuated by laughter, then they seemed to reach an agreement and the officer turned back to her.

"On your feet!" he barked suddenly. She jumped up. "Over there!" He pointed at the pillar on which was the mirror.

Clutching her hands to her private parts, Lia hurried across. She could see the blond man watching her and that, somehow, gave her strength. The officer walked up close so that he towered over her, his deputy following.

"Are you carrying any weapons?"

Lia almost laughed. How could she possibly be carrying weapons in her state? She shook her head.

"The Law empowers me to search you," he said. "Up against that pillar. Now!"

Lia stared at him. Surely he couldn't be serious? "But I..."

Thwack! The officer had drawn his night stick and brought it down hard across her buttocks, so that she squealed in surprised pain.

"The pillar!" he barked.

Lia turned and faced the mirror, then slowly removed her hands from her body and placed them against the glass. The reflected sight of her exposed body mocked her, and the sea of excited and grinning faces behind her confirmed she remained the unwilling centre of attention.

"Open your legs." She obeyed. "Wider!" She felt the night stick roughly shoving her legs apart. She stretched them as wide as she could, spreading her arms apart above her head, trying not to look at the reflection of her body before her.

In the mirror she saw the officer replace his stick in his belt, then move close behind her.

At first his touch was soft, the large rough hands running over her as if a genuine search was in progress. He ran his hands down her arms, first one then the other. Then the hands came round her neck, caressing her smooth shoulders and reaching round to touch her face.

The hands slid down her back slightly and ran under her arms, reaching around, stroking the soft globes of her breasts and coming to rest on her nipples. The man began to work her nipples between finger and thumb. She gasped with the pleasure of the sensation and was ashamed to see the tips go hard and firm under his touch, so that they stood out, as if with a pride that she did not share. He squeezed them gently and she let out an involuntary moan of gratification, causing the crowd to murmur expectantly. He continued this treatment for some time, and Lia began breathing deeply as she felt her juices flowing again.

Suddenly the hands left her breasts and she gave a small sigh of disappointment. She felt him run his fingers down her back, his thumbs tracing her spine. His hands moved lower to her buttocks, squeezing and caressing, his nails lightly scratching their perfect rounded surface.

She glanced in the mirror and saw him crouch. Then he was feeling her ankles, the same firm but gentle touch. He caressed her calves, up the backs of her legs, then began stroking her inner thighs. He worked up higher and her stomach knotted in anticipation of the inevitable destination. She felt his fingers press on the soft lower curve of her buttocks, and his thumbs slid into the deep valley between them, making her draw breath sharply.

The thumbs worked further, kneading the flesh and pulling the two globes aside so that she knew her puckered anus was revealed. He ran a fingertip over it, then down again, teasing her pubic hair at the point where her slender legs met.

Lia was gripped by an overwhelming desire and the warmth and wetness in her belly increased. Why didn't he come through between her legs and reach the very point of her lust? Why was he just tormenting her? Desperately, almost without control, she began thrusting her rear back against his hand, her hips circulating in a lewd gyration which betrayed her wanton desires. From behind her she could hear the comments of the watchers.

"Christ, she's a hot one."

"Just look at that lovely arse."

"I bet she'd take on the lot of us."

Then the touching stopped completely. "Turn around." The order was pronounced more softly, and the crowd was silent and expectant.

Lia removed her hands from the mirror, the sweaty imprints left behind betraying the tension she was feeling. With difficulty she brought her legs together and turned. Her face was flushed with shame and excitement. She shouldn't be allowing this to happen to her. She looked down to see her nipples firm and erect, as if in defiance of her own wishes. She knew that, despite the fact it hadn't been touched, her clitoris was swelling. She hoped it didn't show.

"Hands back on the mirror, above your head. Lean back. Get those legs apart. Wider."

Desperately she struggled to obey. Something in his authoritative manner attracted her. She desired to please him and didn't care that she was being watched. What had Perce called her? Horny little slut, that was it. Perhaps he was right. All she knew was that she had to obey.

She reached above her head until her palms came into contact with the mirror. She spread her legs, bending her knees and thrusting her hips forward, so that her vagina was open and accessible. The crowd murmured again and there was a scraping of chairs as men stood to get a better look.

A camera flashed from somewhere in the room. Lia imagined what the shot would look like. A lovely young woman, totally nude, her back arched, her breasts thrust upwards under tension, the dark nipples hard and prominent, her hips deliberately projected as if to offer her open sex to anyone who wanted it. Her thoughts went to the magazines in her boss's drawer, with its photos of women.

Surely none of their poses were as provocative, as totally sexual as the one she was being forced into? She wondered if the man would masturbate over the picture, and found herself hoping he would. She wanted him to have it enlarged and framed and hung in a place of honour above the bar so that all those who visited would see her naked charms so wantonly displayed and regret not being present on this momentous day.

The officer's hands were on her body again, teasing her nipples, squeezing her breasts, kneading and stroking. Then inevitably his hands moved down, over her taut ribcage, down her tummy, fingers stroking through her pubic hair, gently easing apart the outer lips and exposing the pink wetness within.

She stared into his craggy face as if challenging him to go further. He took hold of her clitoris, rolling it between his fingers, feeling it swell as she emitted a cry of surprise and lust. She felt him move his hands aside, pulling at the outer lips again, and she knew he was showing the other men her wet love bud as proof of her arousal. The camera flashed again.

And then his hands were back at work, fingers thrusting deep into her vagina, causing her to contract her inner muscles around them, caressing them as if they were the penis of some invisible lover who had chosen to strip her and fuck her in this public place. Her breath was coming in shorter bursts, and she knew that if he didn't stop soon she would suffer the humiliation of an orgasm in front of a group of complete strangers.

Then suddenly he did stop. He withdrew his fingers and stood back, watching the flushed girl as she fought to bring her writhing body back under control; legs wide apart, hips pumping, her head thrown back, her breath coming in short bursts, the sweat that ran down between her breasts glistening.

At last the panting eased and her senses began to return.

The officer spoke at last. "I don't think she's armed."

The room rang with raucous laughter and Lia shut her eyes. Her desires now having subsided, feelings of shock and shame began to overcome her.

"However," the officer continued above the noise, "I still have a few questions I'd like to ask. Is there somewhere we can be alone?"

A cheer and shouts of laughter went up from the onlookers, and Lia felt a strange hollow sensation in her stomach. She already had a fairly shrewd idea about the form the questioning would take and was surprised at the mixed feelings it aroused in her.

The barmaid pushed through the crowd. She stood in front of Lia, her eyes wandering up and down her helpless body. "There's always the games room." The irony of the statement was not lost on the crowd, who gave another cheer. The barmaid reached out and ran her hand up the inside of Lia's thigh to where, much to Lia's intense embarrassment, a trickle of moisture had escaped her vagina. The girl rubbed it between finger and thumb. "Don't make a mess of the pool table though."

The crowd laughed and Lia tried to turn away to hide her shame. She felt her arm grabbed roughly and staggered upright.

"Put your hands behind your head," the officer ordered. She obeyed, clasping her fingers together behind her neck, so that her breasts jutted forward invitingly.

The officer swung her round and pointed to a door beside the bar. "In there." He thrust her forward, into the mass of onlookers. They stayed put, obliging her to push through them. They winked and leered as she passed, some making obscene gestures, others reaching out to touch her bare flesh, pinching her arse or tweaking her nipples. She gazed straight ahead, keeping her hands clasped as she had been told, making no attempt to stop them.

At last she reached the doorway and stepped through, relieved to be free of their clutches.

Chapter Four
Officers' Perks

The room was a lot smaller than the one she had just left, though it shared the dirty lino floor and the harsh strip lighting above. In the centre stood a pool table, the cloth faded and stained with years of use. All around the walls were video games machines that flashed and bleeped occasionally. The walls were hung with photos cut from old calendars, depicting nude or semi-nude women in various provocative poses. She wondered if they had ever been looked on by a live naked woman before. The thought amused her and she reflected again on the man who had been photographing her. It now seemed certain to her that her own photo, or photos, would soon adorn this room, and a good deal more provocative they would be than these tame offerings of girls in studios, where a wisp of pubic hair would have seemed risqué. She stretched her body up proudly and turned to face the door, her hands still behind her head. The immediate passion of the scene in the bar had receded, but she still retained the warmth in her belly and she knew it would not take much to rekindle her desires.

The officer took longer than she expected to come in, and she waited anxiously for his arrival. She wondered whether he expected her to prepare for his questioning in any way, but decided to await orders.

At last he appeared. He paused momentarily in the doorway, taking in her body as she stood patiently waiting. Then he closed the door firmly behind him. The room seemed strangely quiet as the hubbub from outside was cut off, and with just the two of them together a strange shyness overcame her. Suddenly he spoke.

"Why are you naked?"

"They wouldn't give me any clothes." She cast her eyes down, embarrassed by the subject.

"You mean you were naked when they found you?"

She nodded.

"Where were you?"

"I was on the highway, trying to hitch a ride."

"You were trying to hitch a ride stark naked?"

"Yes."

"Didn't you know what was likely to happen? Most of these bloody drivers would have fucked the arse off you as soon as look at you."

She blushed at his coarse language. "I'd lost my clothes. It was an accident." She started to explain, but he seemed to have lost interest.

"Sit on the edge of the pool table."

The order took her by surprise, but she turned obediently and lifted herself up so that her backside rested on the edge, replacing her hands behind her head.

"Lie back, and open your legs." She had become an object again. Something to be played with, to be abused. Obediently she lay back, her shoulders resting on the baize of the table. Slowly she spread her legs apart, as wide as she could. The raised edge of the table caused her body to arch automatically, making her pose even more provocative.

He began caressing her again, opening her labia and stroking her intimately. She moaned softly.

"They whip you there?" he asked suddenly.

She was taken unawares. "What?" she mumbled lamely.

"There. That wet little love pocket that you're so keen to flash to all and sundry. And don't deny it. When that guy in there started takin' pictures you was showin' it like some two-bit whore."

"I... I'm not a whore. I just can't help..." Her voice trailed away.

"Answer my question. Ever been whipped there?"

"No."

"Well, I reckon after your little exhibition in there it's about time. After all, prancing about the highway in the buff in broad daylight's a pretty serious offence. There's indecent exposure, soliciting, causing a disturbance. I guess a good whipping is in order."

She was aghast. Surely no one would whip her there. Even though she had behaved like a cheap slut on the highway, and afterwards in the diner, would he really do that to her? She watched anxiously as he began to unravel the thong that held the bottom of his holster to his leg. It was made of shiny leather, about half an inch thick and eighteen inches long. He folded it in two, wrapping the double end around his fingers. Lia lay there, too scared to move, yet aware that in her present position she was offering him a perfect target.

He began caressing her again with his left hand, and again she found her legs trying to open still further to envelop his hands.

Crack! The thong bit savagely into her inner thigh, making her shout with pain. Then his left hand returned and continued its intimate caresses.

Crack! This time on the other side. She writhed beneath the onslaught, not daring to close her legs, despite the stinging pain of the blow. His left hand returned, the fingers penetrating her, feeling the wetness within.

Crack! Once again she cried out loud. She knew the sound of the punishment and her cries would be audible outside in the diner, and she wondered what they would be thinking.

Crack! Her sex was burning with the pain of the beating, but still she kept her legs apart, relishing the intervals between the strokes when he would continue to stimulate her tortured sex.

Crack! The thong fell again, this time across her front so that the mark ran down her belly and was lost in the bush of her pubic hair.

The punishment continued, first the tender caresses, then the fierce stroke across her sex, so that soon she was finding it difficult to distinguish the pain from the pleasure, thrusting towards the thong as it lashed down, as well as to his caresses. She felt the juices flowing within her once more, despite herself.

A knock sounded at the door.

"Come!" he called. Crack! The thong came down again. The door opened. It was the barmaid holding a tray with two bottles and glasses. So that was what had kept him when she was waiting for him in the room.

"Where do you want these?" The girl was grinning as she caught Lia's eye.

Crack! "On the table."

The girl sauntered across and Lia realised she had deliberately left the door wide open. Lia was lying in such a position that her open, punished sex was directly facing the doorway so that when she raised her head and peered through the valley between her breasts she could see the crowd, craning for a view of her latest humiliation.

Crack! Again the thong lashed down, making her moan out loud. Then the left hand took over again, manipulating her red and swollen lips, making her arse grind against the edge of the table in her exquisite discomfort. Meanwhile the girl was taking her time, pouring the drinks and, along with the men, enjoying the show.

Crack! He struck her again, then paused, turned to the open door and ran his fingers down the length of the thong. Drops of moisture fell to the floor, and more followed as he shook it. Lia watched the fascination on the men's faces.

"Anything else?" The barmaid was lingering, determined that Lia's punishment would be public for as long as possible. The officer shook his head. She backed to the door, hesitating before closing it, allowing the men one final view.

Crack! Lia was getting frantic now, wanting the punishment to end, yet in a state of total sexual arousal. Crack! A squeal came involuntarily from her lips. Would this never end? She understood now that she had been foolish to allow herself to be captured naked, and that her wanton behaviour in the bar was worthy of punishment, but surely she had been punished enough?

Crack! Her whole body shuddered as the thong fell. Then suddenly it stopped. She saw that the officer had dropped the thong. He was standing back, swigging his beer, studying her.

"Get up." She rose unsteadily and dropped down onto her feet, taking care to keep her hands behind her head and her legs apart.

"Down there." The officer gestured to the floor.

Lia looked for something on which to lie. There was nothing. The floor was filthy with dirt, spilt beer and cigarette ash.

She knelt down, then lowered herself to the floor. The lino felt cold against her back and arse and the grit dug into her. The smell of stale tobacco was stronger down there. Somehow lying on the floor, the bare linoleum, she felt even more exposed than ever. Other women had sex in warm rooms, on beds with bedclothes, a sheet to cover their modesty whilst awaiting their partner, the prospect of making soft love, followed by a sleep in their lover's arms. Lia was lying stark naked on the filthy floor of a sleazy diner waiting to be fucked by a complete stranger. And the thought of it made her excited! She was actually enjoying it!

The officer knelt between her legs. His hands went to the belt of his trousers and he began to unbuckle it.

Lia watched. Yes, she thought, this is the fate of one such as me. No glamorous affairs, no romance, just a horny slut being screwed by whoever's strong enough to take her. No foreplay, just a beating, then an erect cock.

The officer had lowered his pants to his knees and she could see the final weapon of her punishment. Thick and erect with a glistening end, like some great sword about to pierce her. She spread her legs wider and pressed her feet on the floor, lifting her hips and offering her open vagina. She was ready to be penetrated.

The man leant over her, she felt his hot breath on her face. She felt too the tip of his penis nudging against the entrance to her love hole. Taking her hand momentarily from behind her head she reached down for his weapon, guiding it to the entrance of her pussy.

Then, with a thrust, he was inside her and she cried out in ecstasy as she felt him penetrate her. At first just the tip of him was inside her, probing gently, working slowly at her, causing her muscles to contract and relax with its rhythm. She felt him push harder, each stroke carrying him a little further inside, deeper and deeper.

She responded to his movements with her own, trying to match him push for push, gyrating her hips in a slow, regular rhythm, contracting her muscles to squeeze his cock, as if sucking him further into her.

He began thrusting more fiercely, with an increasing momentum. The buttons on his jacket were pressing into her breasts, and his bristles scratched her face, the linoleum hard against her backside, but she didn't care. All that mattered to her was the cock in her cunt.

Harder he pumped. She could feel his balls slapping against her. He lifted himself for a moment and she knew he was admiring her nakedness.

Then suddenly he withdrew and she let out a cry of disappointment.

"On your hands and knees," he ordered.

She scrambled to obey him, taking up the position with her back to him.

"Lift your arse."

She crouched forward on her elbows, forcing her backside back and up at him, straining back so that the globes of her arse were stretched taut, revealing her anus and below it her sex, glistening with wetness. She strained to open her legs as wide as she could, offering herself to him unashamedly.

He moved closer, and once again she felt his penis as he ran it down the crack in her arse, pausing to stroke the puckered hole before once again probing at her vagina.

Lia pushed back against him, willing him to penetrate her. Still he hesitated. Lia could stand it no longer.

"Fuck me!" she shouted. "For God's sake fuck me!"

Smack! His hand came down hard on her arse. "Ask again!"

She felt tears rise in her eyes, her backside smarted with the pain. "Please fuck me," she pleaded.

Smack! His hand struck again, this time on the other cheek. "You're a foul-mouthed little bitch. What are you?"

"A foul-mouthed little bitch," she sobbed.

"And what do you want?"

"Your cock inside me."

Suddenly he was pushing into her again and she thrust backwards urgently, emitting a hoarse moan of pleasure as she felt him enter her. "Yes, yes!" she screamed as he rammed his rod home.

He took up a regular rhythm once again, gripping her thighs and driving into her violently. She struggled to keep her balance as he shook her body with his pounding. Her breasts hung beneath her, swaying back and forth as she crouched on the filthy floor.

His actions were becoming frenzied and her arse was slapping against his stomach as he shafted her. Then suddenly she felt him stiffen and knew he was about to come. Surely he wouldn't climax so soon? If only he would take a little longer. Then before she knew it he was spurting into her. She wanted to shout that she wasn't ready. But already she could feel his rhythm breaking as his seed continued to fill her vagina. His motions began to slow, even as she attempted to shove more urgently against him. And then he was withdrawing. She tightened her muscles about his organ, willing him to continue, to finally take her over the top too. But he pulled out, ignoring her desire, and she crouched, almost crying with frustration as she gazed back at his penis, wet with her juices, the semen still oozing from its tip.

He shoved her onto her back and leaned over her once more, wiping the sperm from his organ onto her pubic hair in a gesture of utter contempt, then stood up and began pulling up his pants.

And as she watched she understood. The punishment had been for her, the sex had been for him. No one cared whether she was satisfied. She was just an object to be abused and discarded.

"Get up." She rose to her feet, brushing her arse and back in a futile effort to remove the dirt. "Drink this." He thrust a glass of beer into her hand, and she realised he had ordered one of the drinks for her. It was the first act of kindness anyone had shown her since her capture and she felt somehow touched by the gesture. She swigged the liquor urgently, realising how thirsty she was. It spilled from the sides of her mouth and dribbled down her chin, causing a trickle between her breasts, but she didn't mind.

"Wait here." He left her standing by the pool table finishing the beer, went out and closed the door behind him. She was alone for a few moments with her thoughts and fears. She wondered what would happen next. Clearly the ordeal was not yet over. She put down the glass and gazed at the pool table. She even considered taking a few shots, then realised that she had no money. In fact she had nothing at all. Not a thing. She was completely at the mercy of those outside. She reached down and touched her sex. The wetness of her own juices had mingled with the officer's sperm and was leaking, running down her legs. She looked about for something to wipe it away. Then the door opened.

The deputy!

She should have guessed that he also would want his share. Until now he had remained in the background, just an interested onlooker. She recognised that he was somewhat shy compared with his boss, that he had been unsure up until then. She guessed he had been cowed by the presence of the senior man. But he had been left alone while his superior was taking his pleasure, had been encouraged by the crowd while waiting for his return, and now he had clearly asserted himself. If his boss was allowed to take his pleasure, at least he expected something for himself.

Lia reacted instinctively, placing her hands behind her head and opening her legs, felt the sperm oozing from her once more. She stood still and waited for him to approach her. Now that she had given herself so entirely to his superior, somehow she feared the deputy less. Let him do what he would with her; she had proved herself worthy.

He approached her slowly. Without the crowd behind him he was clearly less sure of himself. She found herself feeling sorry for him. She realised he needed some encouragement, but she was unsure what more she could do.

He stood in front of her, hesitating. At last he spoke. "Have you ever given a man oral sex?"

She knew what he meant, she'd read magazines and books, but she had never been asked before.

"No," she replied.

"Well I want you to give me oral sex." He spoke as if it was some kind of prescription from the doctor.

"All right."

He seemed surprised at her compliance. As if he had expected her to refuse. She almost wished she had, if only to see what he would have done next. But the thought of tasting this quiet young man's cock, of bringing him to orgasm, of giving him what the majority of the men outside would have taken without asking if not for the power of the Bikers, all of these things made her want to do as he ordered.

Without further ado she dropped to her knees, reaching for his belt. She undid it slowly, enjoying the moment as his hands reached down and began fondling her breasts. She unbuttoned his pants and slowly pulled down his zip. They dropped to his ankles and she reached for his briefs, yanking them from him and revealing his penis. It was stiff and erect standing proudly in front of her face. She reached for it eagerly. She had never seen one at such close range, and she was anxious to examine it, feel it, stimulate it.

Her hands closed about the deputy's cock. It was uncircumcised and she slid back the foreskin, running her fingertips gently over the glans, fascinated by the way it made the whole organ stiffen still further. She reached beneath, cupping his balls, weighing them in her hands and caressing them gently. The deputy grunted with pleasure and she felt her womb tighten deliciously with the prospect of his orgasm.

She pulled his organ closer to her face, rubbing her hand up and down it with an increasing rhythm. Then she opened her mouth and took him in, just the tip at first. She ran her tongue round the swollen end, licking under the foreskin whilst still gently masturbating him with her hands. The smell and the taste of his manhood aroused her, and she longed for a hand or a cock to stimulate her own sex.

Unable to restrain herself any longer she opened her mouth and took him deep inside. His cock filled her and she sucked hungrily at it, moving her head back and forth with an increasing rhythm. She found her own desire rise, the very act of satisfying him somehow fulfilling. She thrust her head back and forth with a new vigour, enjoying the feel of the thick penis between her lips.

His excitement was increasing and he began thrusting his hips against her, literally fucking her eager face. She sucked at his organ with relish as he pumped at her, his balls slapping her chin, which was wet with her own saliva. He took hold of her hair, slamming her head against him, making her bare breasts bounce with the force of his onslaught, beating against his legs, causing the nipples to harden as they were stimulated by the motion. She wanted to laugh and cry at the same time, happy to be so abused, ready to accept his seed, knowing he would boast to his companions of his dominance over her, how he'd had his way so easily.

She felt him become tense, his buttocks clenching where she held him, and she sucked all the harder on his stiff rod as it slipped in and out of her mouth.

Then with a groan he reached his climax and she felt the semen spurt into her. It struck the back of her throat, causing her to gag momentarily, so that his cock slipped from her lips, still pumping copious streams of sperm into her face, her hair. Frantically she grabbed at it, cramming it back into her mouth, anxious not to lose any more of its precious contents, sucking in time with his spurts, draining him greedily, swallowing his seed as he continued to thrust at her face, his movements slowing, his eyes closed, his head back, until at last the movements ceased.

Lia continued holding him between her lips, sucking out the last vestiges of his orgasm. Finally she slid her head slowly back, reluctant to let him go. She caressed the wilting organ, licking it clean. Then she sat back on her ankles, her hands behind her head again, awaiting her next orders.

As the deputy pulled up his pants and fastened them he watched her lick the sperm from round her mouth, like a child that had just finished a particularly messy ice cream.

"You're quite a cock-sucker," he said at last. She smiled slightly, pleased with the compliment. Some women were great secretaries, others could cook wonderful meals, but she was quite a cock-sucker, and that seemed a good qualification in her current predicament.

"On your feet!" he ordered suddenly, and she sprang to obey. "Now back outside."

She walked towards the door, apprehensive. If she had looked a sight before, what did she look like now? She paused before another mirror. What she saw did not encourage her.

Her hair was a mess, tangled and matted with the deputy's sperm. There was more sperm on her cheeks and on her chin, from which a trickle of it could be traced down her neck to her right breast, where a glutinous blob hung precariously from her nipple, which was still proudly erect. Her pubic hair too was soaked and another trail ran down from her sex almost to her ankle. Her knees and elbows were dirty from the floor, and half turning she could see that her buttocks and shoulders were similarly grimy, here and there a brown patch of spilt beer or a scrap of cigarette ash giving a blotchy effect. The insides of her thighs bore marks of the whipping, and served to draw attention to the lips of her vagina, swollen partly from the punishment, partly from her lust. The thought of re-entering the diner filled her with apprehension.

She glanced at the deputy, back in his pants and looking none the worse, and felt the contrast. If only she had some clothes, something at least to cover the evidence of her ravishment. Even somewhere to wash would have helped. But she had neither, so taking a deep breath she walked to the door and stood waiting, hands clasped obediently behind her head - naked, dirty, unable to control the arousal that was evident in her breasts and her sex, and about to be exposed to a roomful of lurid men.

As the door was opened she felt the room go silent as eyes turned to her. The diner was fuller than ever, with more truckers arriving and those already there reluctant to leave while she was still around. Lia looked at the deputy, who gestured her out. She took a deep breath, then stepped into the room.

There was a scraping of chairs as they craned for a better look. Lia felt her face burn as she walked into full view, followed by the deputy. She had intended to walk proudly, head erect, but she felt her nerve beginning to desert her in the face of the crowd. Across the room she could see the Bikers, still at their table, apparently unconcerned at her entrance.

She made her way between the crowded tables, looking neither right nor left, intent on her destination. At last she arrived at the place where the bikers sat, talking unconcernedly amongst themselves. She took up a position beside the table, hands behind her head and legs apart, with her back to the room, and waited.

At last Perce turned to her. His eyes travelled up and down her body as he took in her condition.

"Christ, you're a mess," he said at last. "What the hell have you been doing?"

"You know," she muttered.

"Sorry?" He was putting on his deaf act again and her heart sank as she realised he intended to humiliate her still further.

"You know what happened," she said again.

"How could we?" he asked in a mocking tone. "You've been in the games room all this time. I think you should tell us how you got into that state. In fact, I think everyone would like to hear."

Hadn't they had enough? She watched in apprehension as Perce got up from his seat and walked to the centre of the crowded room. He spoke to a group sitting there, who quickly cleared their glasses from their table, clearly in awe of the Biker's powers. Then he beckoned to her. Her heart heavy with dread, she moved to him.

"Up on the table," he ordered.

"What?"

"Up on the table. Now!"

She looked around for an empty chair to step up on, but there were none. She grasped the edge of the circular metal table and began clambering on, aware of how awkward she must appear. Soon she was crouching on all fours in the middle of the table.

"Stand up."

Slowly, unsteadily, she got to her feet. Once she had gained her balance she took up her subservient stance, legs apart and hands behind her head. In her elevated position she felt completely exposed. Her sex was now in full view of all in the room. Two or three more flash bulbs went off around the room, and she reacted by thrusting her pubis forward and throwing back her shoulders in proud defiance.

Perce spoke again. "Now then, tell us all what happened. How did you get those stripes on your thighs?"

"I... it was the officer." She scanned the room for him, but there was no sign, and through the window she could no longer see his vehicle. Then to her dismay she realised that the other Bikers had left too, and along with them her blond prince. She felt glad in a way, that he would not witness her further degradation, but at the same time it seemed to her as if her only ally had deserted her.

"Go on."

"He... he whipped me there."

"Where?"

"Between my legs."

"Where?"

"He... he whipped my cunt." She paused, deeply embarrassed by having to use the word. "He made me lie on the pool table with my legs apart. Then he whipped my cunt with a leather thong."

"What happened next?"

"He made me lie down on the floor, on my back. Then he... he took me."

"He took you? Where?"

"No. He... he just took me."

"Tell us what you mean, slut."

"He fucked me."

"What, in the middle of the pool room? On that filthy floor? You just let him fuck you?" Perce was enjoying himself. "Tell us exactly how he did it."

And so Lia was forced to give a detailed account of her ordeal, describing how she had raised her hips to guide him in, and how he had driven into her, how she knelt on her hands and knees and begged him to take her, how he came inside her. And all the time she was telling them the memory returned vividly and she found her juices beginning to flow again.

She went on to describe how she had brought the deputy to orgasm, and as she did so the lust in her increased and she felt her nipples harden, even without physical stimulus. As she recalled the taste of the cock in her mouth the lips of her sex began to swell and she knew her clitoris was becoming more prominent. She felt as if the sea of eyes were physically caressing her body, and her vagina began to convulse as if tightening round an imaginary cock. She knew the men could see her arousal, but was unable to contain herself.

"And what's that all over your face?"

"It's sperm."

"What, all over your face? And it's on your tit. Look at her tit, lads. That's sperm on it. That's disgusting, isn't it guys? Going round like that?" He looked up at her. "Lick it off."

"What?"

"Do as I tell you."

Blushing scarlet, she removed her hands from her neck. Taking hold of her right breast she pulled it up to her mouth, then craning down her neck, she began to lick, working her way to the nipple. The taste of the sperm and the sensation of her tongue on her breast stimulated her and she found herself thrusting her pelvis lewdly as the muscles in her vagina undulated.

"Keep licking. Lick the other one now. That's right." The cameras flashed again. She began to lose control as the licking aroused her. Her left hand slipped down and began caressing her clitoris, pulling aside her sex lips in a spontaneous reaction to the cameras.

Her hips were moving harder and she moaned as she continued to stimulate both breast and vagina. She bent her knees, holding them wide apart. She sensed the atmosphere of hushed expectation, the men craning forward for a better look at her. Oblivious to all but her own uncontrolled desires she thrust three fingers deep into her sex, moving them in and out in rhythm with her gyrating hips.

Her breath began coming shorter, and with each exhalation she gave a grunt of passion. The eyes of the men had become a stimulus for her, the thought of her nudity, herself gratification, her sheer exhibitionism redoubling her abandoned passion.

She began to turn herself round, moving from one foot to the other in order to ensure that everyone got a close view as she masturbated. She wanted everyone in the room to enjoy the sight. She was approaching her climax and her passion overcame her.

Something cold and hard touched her leg and she looked down to see the barmaid. The girl was holding an empty whiskey bottle in her hand. As Lia watched she stroked its narrow neck in a gesture the significance of which was clear. She offered the bottle up to Lia, who took it uncertainly. The room was hushed as the men craned forward to watch. Lia held it by its thick stem and began running her hand up and down the neck, feeling its surface with a sensuous touch, her fingers caressing the cap as they would a penis. She brought it up to her breasts, rubbing it over her erect nipples, enjoying the sensation of the cold glass on her sweating body. She lifted it to her face, still stroking the stem, and gazed quizzically at it, before opening her mouth and taking it between her lips, sucking it suggestively as she had the deputy's cock.

Her hand slid back to her sex while she sucked, her head down, her eyes scanning the crowd. Her fingers found her love bud once more, caressing it while sucking greedily at the bottle, saliva escaping from the sides of her mouth and running down her chin.

She slid the bottle from her lips and ran it down her neck, through the valley between her breasts and on down her body, a wet trail of saliva marking its path to her swollen clitoris, where she held it for a moment, rubbing gently.

She pressed the cold neck between her legs, forcing the lips of her sex apart so that it disappeared inside her. She gasped as she felt its cool hardness entering her so intimately. For a moment she left it there, rotating it slightly, first one way and then the other, teasing her spellbound audience. But desire overcame her. She wanted it completely inside her, penetrating as far as it would go.

She pressed it further, still rotating it as it worked its way inside, the wet walls of her vagina and the smooth surface of the glass allowing it to slide in easily. She gave a moan of pleasure, the muscles of her vagina contracting instinctively as the thick stem violated her body. She pushed even harder, hungry for its stiff neck to fill her entirely.

The bottle was all the way in now and she once again began to turn around, so that all those watching could see as she worked it gently back and forth with a steady rhythm. Her eyes were closed, her head back, a gentle moan of pleasure escaping her lips as she stimulated herself. The bottle slid in and out, its neck wet with her juices and the officer's sperm.

Her movements began to grow faster as her desire increased. She was close to the edge. Her body was stiff, the veins in her neck standing out as she drove her hips against the bottle. She was panting hard, emitting short harsh screams, her breasts bouncing with the violence of her passion. She knew she was completely the centre of attention, that every prick in the room was hard, desiring to take the place of the bottle in her hot wet vagina. The thought of that was enough. She paused for a second as she reached the peak, then her orgasm was upon her as she cried out with unrestrained lust, juices filling her vagina as she pumped her hips against the uncompromising bottle, oblivious of the audience, of her sheer brazenness in bringing herself to orgasm so publicly.

Her movements slowed and she sank to her knees, legs still apart. She sat back on her ankles, the muscles of her vagina convulsing round the bottle. She continued working it in and out for a while as the spasms subsided, then released her grip and let it rest on the table, its neck still deep inside her. At last she threw back her head, wiped the sweat from her brow and looked about.

For a moment the room was completely silent. Even the barmaid was transfixed, her eyes glued to the naked young woman who sat on the table, breathing heavily from her exertions. Lia gazed into the men's faces with satisfaction as she sat; dirty, dishevelled and utterly exhausted.

Whack! She yelped as Perce's belt cracked across her backside. At once she came back to the reality of where she was and what she had been doing. As her passion ebbed shame and humiliation took its place. She looked down at the bottle that protruded from her sex lips. She reached down and, taking it in both hands, gently slid it from her, the neck making a squelching sound as it was removed. Then her hands went to the back of her head and she stood up on the table again, doing her best to keep as still as she could.

"That's enough of that, you friggin' nympho," Perce spat. "You're bloody insatiable. I think we may have to send you to the Black Cat for a night if you're not careful."

The Black Cat? Was it some form of punishment? She hung her head, wishing she had more control over her passionate body.

"It's time you cleaned yourself up," said Perce. "You can't go around all day looking like you've been shagged by the entire marine corps." He turned to the barmaid, who had recovered her composure and was watching with amusement. "You got a shower or something?"

The girl shook her head. "If you ask me the bitch wants hosing down. Might just be the way to get her off heat. We got a hosepipe in the parking lot."

Perce grinned. "Good idea." He turned to Lia. "Outside in the parking lot, and get a move on."

Lia jumped down from the table and made for the exit, anxious to avoid another stroke from the belt. She pushed the door and stepped out into the sunshine. A truck was just pulling up and its occupants sounded their horn and shouted out at the sight of her.

The barmaid took her by the elbow and dragged her across to a corner of the lot where a sign said WATER. She stood Lia in the concrete bay, where she waited as the crowd gathered round.

All of a sudden a stream of water shot from the nozzle, catching Lia in the stomach. She gasped with the force of the jet and the coldness of the water as it splashed off her, running down between her thighs.

The girl redirected the hose onto Lia's breasts as she stiffened with the shock of it, her nipples shrinking into hard little nuts. She closed her eyes as the spray lifted to her face, splattering against her cheeks and soaking her hair. At the girl's order she turned around, bending over so that the water could be directed straight at her arse, the jet playing off her anus and flushing out the sperm from her vagina.

Someone threw her a bar of soap and she set about removing the grime and semen from her punished skin. She soaped her breasts so that they felt smooth and inviting to the touch, then allowed them to be hosed clean. She scrubbed the dirt from her back and buttocks then, to the cheers of the crowd, washed her sex, standing legs akimbo as the soap was hosed from her.

When she was finally through washing she stood allowing the water to cascade from her body, cold but happy to at least be clean.

Perce snapped an order and the barmaid turned off the hose. Lia remained standing where she was, the chilling water dripping off her, causing her skin to wrinkle with goose bumps as she slowly dried in the sun. Perce led her to a lamppost in the truck refuelling area. Withdrawing a pair of cuffs from his pocket he secured her wrists to a ring, some way up the post so that she strained, just able to touch the ground on tiptoe. The Bikers left her there to dry in the afternoon sun, while they wandered back inside and resumed their drinking.

Lia remained shackled where she was, glad of a moment of solitude, for although she was still being watched she felt confident that none of them would have the temerity to approach her. She closed her eyes, remembering the afternoon, wishing she could reach her breasts and sex and caress herself as she recalled her orgasm. The cuffs chafed her wrists, stretching her body taut, the water trickling from her as she finally began to warm up. She closed her eyes and drifted off into a doze, her punished body relaxed at last as it hung there on display.

She awoke with a start to find herself being released. She gazed about uncomprehendingly. In her daze she forgot her nakedness and stood by as the men gathered round to watch her departure. The Bikers had brought their machines round to where she had been hanging and she was led across to Perce's cycle.

She made as if to climb onto the saddle, but he stopped her. "Other way round," he said with a grin. "Makes a better view." She swung her leg over the seat, and blushed as she felt her legs spread apart while Perce shackled her ankles to the footrests. Then he took her hands and cuffed them together behind her back, locking the cuffs to a ring in the middle of the seat. She was helpless again, facing the rear, her legs apart rendering her visible to all. Perce ran his hands thoughtfully over her breasts and down to her open sex, which he teased for a short time. He was rewarded by the clear signs of arousal.

"Still horny, eh?" he muttered.

Then he was astride the machine. He kicked it into life with a roar, engaged gear and the bikes swept out of the parking lot in a cloud of dust, leaving the onlookers gazing after them, still discussing the afternoon's events.

Chapter 5

The Depot

Once they were back on the open road Lia was able to relax again. She leaned back against Perce, enjoying the motion of the machine as he swept it through the bends, of the vibration of the engine as it resonated through her. The saddle was wide and its leather surface felt good against her bare skin, relaxing her despite her vulnerability. She soon found her body adjusted to the motion, leaning with him as he cornered.

Every now and then they would pass a truck, their high speed far in excess of anything the commercial vehicles could manage, despite their power. As they did so she noticed Perce's tendency to turn in and slow, allowing the truck drivers a delightful view of his naked passenger. At first her reaction was to lower her head and turn away when she was faced with the leering eyes of a lucky driver, but once she realised she was secure in the hands of

52

her captors, that the Bikers were completely in control, she became more confident, so that she was able to stare the drivers in the face, thrusting her hips and opening her legs wide in a bold display.

She began, inevitably, to be stimulated by the throbbing of the machine between her thighs. Riding as she was, naked and exposed, her latent exhibitionism fuelled by the stimulus of the drivers' eyes made her bold. She began staring the truckers straight in the face, licking her lips and blowing kisses, throwing back her shoulders so that her breasts stood out proudly. In reply the men would make lewd signs at her, indicating their desires with crude gestures that made her laugh in the safety of her captivity.

The bikes sped on. The day was warm and Lia felt comfortable where she sat. She began to wonder about where she was being taken. She had heard of the Bikers' bases. Of the areas where the Bikers lived and the trucks were serviced, of how workers were expected to perform as they were instructed. She pondered what her own role could be in such a setup. Looking down at her naked body she guessed it would not be a passive one.

Eventually she realised the bike was slowing, and she watched as the machines behind pulled into single file, so that she was gazing straight into the blind visor of Zep. Suddenly the bike leaned over sharply and they left the highway, following a narrow slip-road that curved round on itself passing underneath the main road, the concrete bridge supports flashing by unnervingly close.

Lia strained round, trying to see where they were going, but all she could make out was the grass by the roadside. She felt the machine braking, throwing her back against Perce. The bike stopped, the other riders drawing to a halt behind Perce's machine. Lia could just discern a high reinforced fence rising on either side. Then came the creak of a gate being opened, a few words exchanged and they were inside the enclosure and moving again.

The service area was large and busy. All around were great trucks in various stages of repair, young men in grease-streaked overalls wielding tools of all descriptions. The fence, which she could see clearly now, was at least twenty feet high and topped with cruel barbed wire. A second fence ran within it with a ditch in between. Escape from this place would be well-nigh impossible.

The Bikers rode on, passed sheds and garages where more trucks stood, their cabs tipped forward to reveal their engines. All around were busy people, hurrying back and forth with tools and spare parts, or leaning over an engine with spanner in hand. And always in evidence were the Bikers, swaggering about shouting orders.

The road began to widen slightly as they rode on, and they swung left into a vast parking area. On one side was a fuelling point, the diesel pumps lined up like sentries awaiting the trucks. Some vehicles were being filled and Lia watched as the attendants snapped back the caps from the fuel tanks and began pumping the liquid in. Then she realised with a shock that the attendants were women. These were the first women workers she had seen and they were all dressed in white overalls, making her feel uncomfortable in her nakedness.

The bikes swung round in a wide arc and came to a halt in front of a low white building with barred windows, Lia no longer able to see the pump attendants. The Bikers switched off their engines and kicked down the stands on their machines before dismounting. Once again it was left to Zep to release the girl from her shackles, and she was soon standing, stretching luxuriously in the sun, her body arched, head thrown back, arms spread wide like some Greek goddess, causing the Bikers to hesitate momentarily while they admired her unashamed display. Lia saw their glances from the corner of her eye, enjoying their admiration, proud of her nudity. She took up her stance, hands behind her head and legs apart, awaiting her next order.

"Inside," said Perce curtly, indicating a door at the front of the building. Obediently Lia entered. Inside it was cool and the contrast from the bright sunlight made it appear dark so she found it difficult at first to see precisely where she was. Gradually she was able to make out a large reception area. It was unfurnished apart from a few chairs that stood against a wall. The carpet was dirty and threadbare and the walls were in need of a coat of paint. At one end stood a desk, behind which sat a girl not much older than Lia, in a grey overall. When she saw Perce she dropped the pen she'd been holding and sprang to her feet. Perce indicated for her to sit down again.

"Vargo in?"

She nodded. Her eyes were fixed on Lia, who stood on display beside Perce.

"Tell him I'd like a word."

The girl came out from behind the desk. As she passed Perce he reached out and grabbed her arm. She swung round and he drew her face to his, kissing her lips. For a second she resisted, then wrapped her arms around him and reciprocated, rubbing her body seductively against him. The embrace went on for some time while Lia stood and watched, somehow embarrassed at being the lone witness to the scene, for the other Bikers had not followed them inside.

At last the two broke apart, the girl stepping back and looking into his face. "Where the hell have you been?" she asked.

"Business."

"What the hell kind of business is she?" the girl said, indicating Lia.

"Just something we found on our travels."

The girl turned and stood in front of Lia, looking her up and down. Lia blushed and lowered her eyes.

"Modest little thing, isn't she?" the girl said, and she and Perce laughed. Lia found herself jealous of their closeness, of their ability to share a joke while she stood silently awaiting her next orders.

Perce patted the girl on the backside. "Now tell Vargo I want to see him, there's a good girl."

With a smile and a wink she was gone, leaving Perce alone with Lia. She felt awkward now, embarrassed at the scene she had witnessed, aware that Perce too was uncomfortable at having betrayed his feelings so openly. She stood facing the empty desk, awaiting the girl's return while he paced up and down impatiently.

At last the girl reappeared. Perce turned to her and Lia sensed he was slightly on edge. He raised his eyebrows.

"He'll see you, but I think he's a bit unhappy about your, er, acquisition."

Perce grunted and pushed past her into the corridor beyond. The girl returned to her desk, where she sat back, her eyes scrutinising the naked captive who stood before her. Lia wanted to talk, to ask questions, but the scene with Perce had made her wary and she was unsure that she could confide in the girl. They remained thus for some time, then the girl spoke.

"You're in my light standing there. Go over by the wall." Lia moved to one side and took up her subservient stance once again, her back to the wall.

The seconds ticked by and became minutes. Half an hour passed and still no sign of Perce. Lia stood without moving while the girl in the overall shuffled papers on her desk. Every now and then the door would open and someone would pass in or out. Some of them were Bikers, but the shabby dress of most betrayed them to be inferiors. Many stopped to gaze at Lia as she stood silently awaiting orders. Some would reach out to touch her breasts or run their hands through her hair, but none were allowed to linger more than a few seconds before the girl would send them on their way with a sharp remark.

The telephone on the desk rang, the loud noise echoing through the hall and making Lia jump. The girl picked up the phone and spoke a few words. Then she replaced it and stood up.

"They want you," she said, and gestured Lia to follow her. They made their way down a long corridor, its decoration as drab as the hall they had just left. At the end was a narrow staircase which they climbed. Lia went first, embarrassed by the close view the girl would have of her bum as they ascended. The girl said nothing.

At the top of the stairs was another long corridor lined with doors, some of them open so that Lia was able to glimpse the workers therein, sitting at desks piled high with paper.

Finally they came to a halt outside one of the doors. It was wider than most, made of polished wood with brass handles; clearly the office of someone with standing.

The girl knocked quietly and without waiting for an answer opened it. Then she took Lia by the elbow and thrust her into the room, closing the door behind her. Lia staggered slightly under the force of the push, then regained her balance. For a moment she forgot herself as she gazed about.

The office was in complete contrast to the corridor she had just left. The walls were hung with expensive flock wallpaper, paintings in large gilt frames adorning them. She stood on a thick expensive carpet that felt soft and springy beneath her bare feet. The room was tastefully furnished with a group of easy chairs in one corner surrounding an occasional table. On the other side of the room was an alcove, its semi-circular walls covered by a series of ten full-length mirrors. Under the window stood a wide mahogany desk behind which sat a man of substantial bulk, his Bikers' leathers slightly incongruous in such a luxurious setting. This, she guessed, was Vargo. Opposite him sat Perce, looking rather more relaxed than when she had last seen him.

"Come here." Lia was shaken from her reverie by the sudden order. Apprehensively she crossed the carpet to where the two men sat. On reaching the desk she stopped, placing her hands behind her head and legs apart, anxious to please the man.

Vargo eyed her up and down for a few moments, then turned to Perce. "Yes," he said, "perhaps I was a little hasty. We may well get a good price." He turned to Lia. "How do you fancy signing a little bit of paper?"

"What is it?"

"An indenture."

"But I thought that was only for," she paused, confused.

"For down and outs?"

"Yes."

"But you are a down and out," he mocked her. "Have you got a job?"

"Well, I did have, but..."

"Exactly. No job. Anyone who would look after you?"

She thought of her blond Biker, but he didn't even have a name she was aware of. Probably he wasn't interested anyway. "No," she said.

"Better sign this then. It says you work for five years, no complaints."

She looked at it. "You haven't filled in who I work for."

"Your new employer will fill that in."

"Or what the wages are."

"They will fill that in too. Now, are you going to sign, freely and without coercion, as it says right here? Or would you rather starve?"

As Lia signed the formidable looking document Vargo looked on with a satisfied grin. Then he turned back to Perce. "She might suit Helda at the Black cat. Let's have a better look. Take her to the alcove."

Perce got to his feet and led her to the wall where the alcove was. She stood facing the mirrors, assailed by the multiple images they reflected back at her. She heard a chair scrape behind her and watched the reflection of Vargo as he crossed the floor towards her. On his feet she saw he was even fatter than she had thought, his gut hanging over the waistband of his trousers.

He reached out, grabbing her by the shoulders and turning her round so that she faced into the room. Then he began the most intimate and personal inspection of her, remarking to Perce as he progressed, but treating Lia as if she wasn't even there.

"Hm, nice hair, could do with a comb though. Eyes are clear enough. All her own teeth. Mouth is a nice size. Sucked the Pig's cock, you said? Looks like a good mouth for cock-sucking. Now let's have a look at these tits. Nice and firm, good nipples, responsive too. You're right, she is a horny little bitch. Let's have a good look at that cunt. Want shaving do you think, or OK as it is? Open your legs. Wider. That's better. Christ she's wet already and I've only been feeling her tits. Now let's see... yes, should fit a good thick cock or two in there. Stop squirming girl, now tighten up, squeeze my fingers, that's it..."

Lia stood as still as she could as the inspection continued, occasionally giving a shudder or uttering a whimper as he handled her. She kept her eyes tightly shut, not wishing to catch Perce's eye as she was mauled, prodded, groped and probed. Her face glowed with shame as she felt the juices flow inside her and heard her captor's remarks on her wetness. If only she could exercise more control over her body. She gasped as she felt her arse cheeks forced apart and a hand slipped between her thighs from behind.

At last the inspection was at an end. All through Vargo had been matter-of-fact, treating her as would a horse dealer examining a prospective purchase. She began to appreciate her standing in this cruel society; just so much flesh to be used to its best purpose. If she were a young man they might be considering her suitability for heavy manual work. As it was, however, she was being considered as a plaything, something to accommodate men's desires. In the end just so much flesh. And yet the girl in the entrance hall, she had been shown affection, been spoken to, even kissed. Clearly it was possible to develop some form of personality, to be treated as a human. She wondered how long it would take.

She stood as they left her, facing the mirrors again, confronted by multiple images of her body, listening to the two men discussing her. It was clear from their conversation that she was not to be kept by them, but to be disposed of at an auction in two or three weeks.

"How are we going to use her in the meantime?"

"We can find something. Maybe the stores or the canteen, or on the pumps."

"OK. Nothing too manual though; don't want to damage the merchandise. Hand her over to Belle. Get her fed and washed and we'll see in the morning."

Perce lifted the receiver and spoke a few words into the phone. Then he replaced it and the men began discussing other business, turning their backs on Lia, as if they had forgotten she was there. Presently there came a knock at the door and it swung open. The girl in the overalls stood there.

"OK Belle. I want her fed and cleaned up and given a bed in your section for tonight. We'll find something for her in the morning."

The girl began undoing the shackles from Lia's wrists. "What about clothes?" she asked.

"What was she wearing when you found her?" Vargo asked Perce.

"Nothing."

"Well we're not running a frigging charity shop. Let her stay as she is; whoever takes her indenture can see to that. Little bitch wants to go around flashing her tits and cunt that's up to her."

Belle grinned. "Might get some of the boys a bit excited," she said.

"Listen, if they've got the energy to fuck sluts like this one we're not working them hard enough. Let them know I said that. Ought to put most of them off."

With that he turned back to Perce and they continued their conversation. Lia, her hands freed, was led to the door and back into the maze of dreary corridors. She followed Belle back down the staircase, but this time they did not return to the entrance hall, leaving the building instead by a small side door. Lia blinked as they stepped into the open air again. The sun was low on the horizon now, but still bright, its colour giving her skin a coppery sheen as she walked behind Belle, her hands clasped obediently behind her head.

They walked for what seemed to Lia some distance, the concrete of the path warm under her feet. They appeared to be taking a route round the back of the buildings, so that they encountered almost nobody. Lia was glad of that, as she had no desire to be seen in her current state and she followed Belle obediently through the warren of buildings that made up the complex.

As they went on the area in which they were walking was becoming more and more deserted, the buildings derelict and unused. Lia was confused. Surely the workers were not housed so far from the main camp? Why was she being brought here?

Suddenly they stopped. They were on a path that ran between two buildings, obviously disused, paintwork shabby, windows broken and hung with cobwebs. Belle led Lia off the path and stood her on the grass with her back to the wall.

"Now," she said, "let's see what we've got. Keep your hands behind your head."

Lia stood obediently, the wall feeling damp and cold on her backside as she waited to see what the girl would do.

Belle began running her hands through Lia's hair, gently at first, teasing the knots out with her long fingers, the movements strangely soothing. Her hands moved to Lia's face, stroking the smooth skin of her cheeks, feeling her features as would a blind person, moving up and down her throat and scratching gently at the nape of her neck, as if stroking a dog. All the time her eyes were fixed on the movements of her own hands, not looking at Lia's eyes at all.

Her hands moved on down Lia's body, circling round her breasts, grasping them gently from beneath, squeezing the soft flesh between thumb and forefinger so that they stood out more prominently than ever. Her fingers probed at the pliant globes, raising and pushing them together. She slapped their undersides gently, clearly pleased with the effect as they quivered, enjoying their young firmness. She ran her hands over them in circular movements, barely brushing the aureoles, all the time intent on what she was doing.

Suddenly, unexpectedly, she spoke. "Being naked like that, it makes you seem so available."

Lia could not think of an answer to that. Certainly it seemed to arouse the lust in those around her. She thought of the diner, and the fascination with her body.

The girl continued playing with Lia's breasts, her voice husky. "When they found you, were you naked then?"

Lia nodded. "I'd lost all my clothes. It was an accident."

"But where were you?"

"I was on the highway. I was trying to get a ride."

"You were hitching a ride, naked? What, just standing there?"

"I was masturbating."

"Frigging yourself?" The girl's voice betrayed an edge of excitement.

"Yes, and caressing my breasts." Lia wasn't sure why she was betraying such intimate details, but she sensed it was what the girl wanted to hear.

"And did anyone stop?"

"Yes." Lia described the truck, how she had stood in the road in front of it, how it slowed and finally stopped. She told Belle about the men inside, how they sat watching her. All the time Belle continued toying with her breasts.

"And you just went on frigging yourself?" Belle was becoming visibly aroused. "Show me. Do it for me like you did it for them." She stood back.

Slowly, reluctantly, Lia stood erect and moved away from the wall. She stood on the concrete path. For a moment she hesitated, gazing round to make sure she wasn't being watched. Then her fingers moved to her breasts, toying with them as she had at the roadside. She slid her hand down between her legs, rubbing gently at first, then sliding her fingers inside, thrusting her hips forward so that the pink slit of her sex was clearly visible. The girl watched in fascination.

"Christ, what a sight. Imagine just doing that. Then in the diner. You were naked there as well? No, don't stop."

Lia went on to describe the happenings in the diner, culminating in her public orgasm on the table, continuing to thrust her fingers into her sex as the girl listened with fascination.

When she had finished, Belle was silent for a while, as if she was wrestling with a decision. When she spoke again her voice had a strange tone.

"Have you ever had a dream, where you're naked in a room full of people, and they're all looking at you?"

Lia nodded, not trusting herself to speak as the action of her fingers was rekindling the desires within her.

"Does that turn you on, being seen by all those people, being exposed, knowing they can see your tits, your cunt, your arse, everything?"

Lia nodded again. "Sometimes." She wondered where the conversation could be leading.

"The point is, you're showing your all, leading them on, making an exhibition of yourself in the most blatant manner, and yet somehow it's safe."

Lia wanted to say that she felt far from safe in her current predicament, but she knew instinctively what the girl meant. Even as she was, it was somehow acceptable that she be nude, and she was aware of her own latent exhibitionism, of the perverse pleasure it gave her to be displayed as she was, available to anyone who wanted to look or to touch, as the girl had done just a few minutes earlier.

"I, I like being watched," she said at last, her eyes cast down. "In the diner, they were taking photographs. That somehow made it even more exciting."

"Photographs? And you posed for them? How?"

Lia stopped masturbating, placing her hands behind her head, widening her legs and forcing her pubis forward, so that the lips of her sex parted, revealing her wet cleft. "Like this."

The girl was breathing heavily, her eyes fixed on Lia's body. "And did that turn you on?" she asked in a trembling voice.

"Very much," said Lia. She hesitated, aware that she might be going too far. "Would you like to display your body naked, Belle?"

The girl lowered her eyes. "Yes," she muttered.

The two were silent for a while and Lia watched her companion, remaining in her provocative pose.

Belle was clearly struggling with a decision. All of a sudden she rose to her feet. She stood, legs apart, hands on hips, staring aggressively at Lia. "Strip me," she said, the authority back in her voice now that the decision was made. "Strip me so that I'm naked like you, so that my tits and cunt are on display."

Lia did not hesitate. The conversation had aroused her and she was anxious to feast her eyes on Belle's charms. Now that she had experienced the touch of another woman she wanted to try it for herself, to feel her breasts, to feast on her body.

She reached for the zipper at the collar of Belle's overalls, sliding it slowly downwards, watching as her throat was revealed, then the rounded breasts, swelling above the lacy bra, the cups cut low, the shape of the nipples outlined against the thin material. She pulled the zipper further, the severe grey material parting to reveal the smooth skin of the belly, the hint of dark hair beneath the navel, extending down into the brief panties that barely covered the pubis.

She eased the garment down Belle's legs, who stood impassive, allowing it to happen. Lia could see the dampness in the gusset of the panties, revealing Belle's desires. Lia eased the overalls over Belle's feet, first one leg then the other, pulling off her slim stilettos as she did so, then carefully replacing them, kissing the feet in a gesture of submissiveness. A final pull and at last the garment was off. She flung it to one side and paused, taking in the sight of the young woman, her hands firmly on her hips, her breasts straining against the meagre bra, the outline of her sex distinct against the skimpy briefs.

Lia pulled Belle to her, their bodies almost touching, breath hot on their cheeks. She reached behind, her fingers working expertly with the catch on the bra, which sprang apart almost immediately. Belle dropped her hands from her hips, letting them hang by her sides, allowing Lia to slide it down her arms. This too she flung to one side carelessly, as if emphasising they had no further need for it. Her eyes were on Belle's breasts, full and rounded, the aureoles large and brown. Lia reached for them, taking one in each hand and squeezing, feeling the warm flesh swell and fill her palms. She felt for the nipples, finding them hard. She played with them, enjoying the feel of their firmness, the puckered brown buds a contrast from the pink softness of the rest of her globes.

Lia bent, about to take the firm teat in her mouth, but a hand grabbed her chin, pulling her face to within an inch of Belle's. The girl looked her in the eye for the first time, speaking through gritted teeth.

"I said strip me!"

Lia stared back into the other's eyes, trying to find some contact, some spark of true communication that would reveal this enigma who held a privileged job, who treated Perce like a lover, who had ready access to Vargo, who was senior enough to be put in charge of a valuable captive such as herself, and who was now asking to be stripped naked, to reveal her charms to anyone who might pass, to be humiliated and exposed. But her search was in vain. The girl lowered her eyes again and stood, hands still by her sides, waiting.

Lia dropped to her knees and reached for the brief panties that were all that covered the girl's modesty. She hesitated for a moment, then hooking her fingers into the flimsy lace she pulled them down her legs. In a single smooth moment she had them down, over the shoes and off, tossed aside as carelessly as the bra. Then she stood back to admire her work.

Belle was slightly taller than Lia, but the high heels she wore made her even taller, her shapely ankles and legs emphasised by the shape of the shoes. Her hair, straight and long, hung down behind her in shining tresses. Her eyes were dark and unresponsive, her lips full and inviting and when she smiled, which in Lia's experience was seldom, she revealed a perfect row of pearly white teeth. Beneath her luscious breasts her body tapered to a trim waist. But it was her sex that held Lia's attention now. The soft, honey-brown triangle of pubic hair had been shaved from the prominent lips, so that they stood out, pink and conspicuous even when her legs were closed. Standing as she was, with legs apart, her vagina was open and inviting, and Lia knew that no man would be able to resist it.

She stood up, unsure of what to do. She longed to take Belle in her arms, to kiss those full lips, to suck those succulent young breasts and to taste the juices in her sex, to press their soft bodies together and make passionate illicit love in this forsaken corner of the camp. She watched the girl's pained expression. She was clearly still struggling with a decision and Lia could see that some primeval desire was rising to the surface; something she was fighting to suppress. At last the girl spoke again.

"Right, now you're the keeper, I'm the captive. You're in charge." Lia watched in fascination as Belle took up the subservient stance that she was becoming so used to.

Lia understood. The talk about dreams, the way she had wanted to know all the details. The girl was playing out a fantasy with her. Her latent desire to expose herself had suddenly surfaced with the arrival of Lia, who was to be kept naked at all times. And at the same time it had given her the opportunity to re-enact the fantasy of her dream, to expose her naked body, if not publicly, at least here, in the open, where the threat of discovery was ever present.

Lia stood for a moment, hesitating, unwilling to displease Belle, yet unfamiliar with the role of dominatrix. How far should she go? She knew Belle's words had, in effect, given her licence to do as she wished, but she found herself reluctant to make the first move. She looked at the girl again. There was a strange passivity about her that gave Lia courage. After all she was the mistress now, and Belle the captive.

She grasped her chin, pulling Belle's mouth to hers and kissing her, letting her tongue probe deep into the mouth of the passive girl. She put her hands behind Belle's head, forcing her closer, pressing her lips hard to her own in a passionate embrace. Belle began to respond, pushing her tongue nervously into Lia's mouth, turning her head to one side and closing her eyes. Lia pulled back, still holding Belle's head in her hands, gazing down at her body. All of a sudden she let go, stepping back.

"Play with your breasts," she said, her voice trembling slightly.

Belle raised her hands. She placed them on her hips for a moment, then slowly ran them up over her waist until they were resting, palms upward, beneath her bosom. Slowly, sensuously, she started rubbing her delectable globes, squeezing them in her palms, pulling them so that they jutted forward as if offering them to her new mistress. She began a gyratory movement with her hands, her fingers circling round her aureoles, squeezing intermittently, emphasising the fullness and pliability of her breasts.

Her fingers closed about her nipples, already hard, projecting invitingly, their darkness against her fair skin making them even more distinct as she stroked them.

Lia was suddenly reminded of the scene in the diner. "Lick your tits," she ordered.

Belle glanced at her quizzically. The idea was clearly new to her.

"Lick your tits I said." Lia was growing in confidence. "Do as I tell you."

Belle grasped her right breast in both hands. She pulled it upwards, squeezing so that it elongated slightly, the nipple standing proud between her hands. Then she bent her neck, projecting her tongue and began licking her breast tip.

Lia watched fascinated as the girl's tongue darted in and out, caressing her nipple and leaving it wet and glistening in the evening sun. She pictured herself doing the same in the diner, and the lust in her began to rise yet again. She pulled Belle over to the wall, standing with her back to it, hands on hips, legs apart. "Caress me," she said.

Belle stared at her for a moment, breathing heavily, her breasts rising and falling in a way which made Lia lick her lips with desire. She reached out, gently stroking Lia's neck, running her hands down and round, under the firm globes of her breasts. Her fingers moved to Lia's nipples, teasing them gently, feeling them respond. Lia drew breath sharply with the exquisite sensation. Belle moved her hands up to Lia's mouth, gently easing her lips apart and sliding her fingers inside. Lia licked the fingers, sucking them in a spontaneous reaction. Then Belle withdrew them and began carefully rubbing the saliva into the dark skin of Lia's nipples, making them glisten with the wetness as they grew more erect.

She continued this sensuous massage for some time, her fingers working the spittle into the flesh like some expensive ointment, so that the buds stood out hard and inviting, as if begging to be sucked.

Belle abandoned Lia's left breast with her hands, and bending placed her mouth over it, sucking gently while her tongue flicked back and forth over the firm nipple, her fingers continuing to stimulate the other, so that it remained erect and prominent.

Lia stood breathing heavily, hands on hips, looking down at the girl who sucked so hungrily at her bare breast. She moaned slightly as she felt the lips abandon her left breast, only to begin again on the right, making her writhe with pleasure. Her mind was a whirl. The softness of touch, the tresses of hair falling over her bare skin, the feminine smell of Belle as she stimulated her all combined in a sensation she had never experienced before. She found herself wanting to hold and suck the firm breasts she could feel warm against her.

Belle continued her attentions on Lia's breasts, sucking greedily, her saliva running down Lia's belly and channelling between her thighs where it mingled with the moistness already gathering there. Then, as if guided by the silvery trail, her hands began to slide downwards, stroking, pausing to gently penetrate her navel before drifting on, over the dark hairs that covered her mound and reaching for her sex lips.

Belle's fingers closed in on their destination from either side, gently easing the lips of her sex apart and feeling the warm wetness inside, stroking back and forth over the smooth surface of the flesh before finding her love button, trapping it between her fingertips, feeling it swell. Lia gasped at the intimacy of the touch, her whole body on fire with desire. The fingers worked on, sliding inside her, feeling the warm wetness within, moving in and out with a regular rhythm that made her moan with pleasure, whilst all the time the girl's lips were clamped on her breasts, sucking noisily.

Lia's mind was a whirl of confusion, unable to come to terms with the strange setting of her ravishment. The derelict buildings, their windows cracked and cobwebbed, their walls damp and grimy, and in contrast the smooth, vital skin of the naked girl, alive with passion, abandoning herself to the wilful caresses of another female in this dingy spot. What a sight she must make! What if someone were to come along, to see her pinned against the wall like some exotic species of butterfly whilst being openly aroused in the most blatantly sexual manner? She found herself looking about, fearful that someone might come by.

Suddenly Belle's lips left Lia's swollen breasts, her tongue licking down her ribcage, working its way over her belly towards the centre of her desires. As her head sank lower Belle dropped to her knees, as if kneeling in adoration before some exquisite goddess, her lips kissing Lia's stomach, her tongue penetrating her navel. The mouth continued its descent, her hands moving down to Lia's thighs, pulling them apart to give her easier access to her inevitable destination. She reached Lia's sex. She hesitated for a moment, studying it, as if planning her assault, then she extended her tongue, probing gently between Lia's nether lips, then licking tentatively at her clitoris, flicking it delicately with her tongue as she had her nipples. Lia drew in her breath sharply, bending at the knees, thrusting her hips forward with the extreme intimacy of the contact, her moaning getting louder.

Belle grew bolder, moving in closer to Lia's crotch, closing her lips around her love bud and sucking it into her mouth, her teeth nibbling gently. Lia let out a shout of pleasure at the sensation. Only her shoulders remained pressed against the wall as she drove her open crotch against the girl's face, heedless of who might see her as she abandoned herself to pleasure.

Belle had a firm grip on Lia's buttocks. She extended her tongue, probing into Lia's vagina, lapping at the wetness as she dragged the naked girl's sex against her face, drinking in the taste and smell of femininity, gripping tightly to maintain her position as Lia's hips thrust against her.

Lia was coming close to her orgasm, the action of Belle's tongue, the open situation and the sheer eroticism of the moment starting to overcome her. She was grunting loudly with each thrust of her hips, her head thrown back and her eyes closed as Belle's tongue continued to explore her open sex. Moisture trickled down her inner thighs, a mixture of saliva and her own juices forming a silvery trail that ran almost to her ankles. She pictured herself standing thus, feet planted wide apart, knees splayed, her breasts, still wet with saliva, tossing up and down to the rhythm of her passion while her companion lapped urgently at her, and imagined being seen, being watched as she had been in the diner, and the image sent her over the edge.

With a scream of release she let her orgasm fill her, the burning pleasure in her thighs becoming the focal point of her whole being as her body was racked with the spasms of her climax. Pushing back against the wall with her shoulders she thrust her hot vagina against Belle's face with an uncontrolled violence, crying out with wanton abandon, careless of who might hear her, while the girl responding by redoubling her efforts with her tongue, delving deeper into Lia's sex, drinking the juices as they flowed, feeling the passion that filled her body.

And then the lust began to ebb as Lia came down from the peak, her movements slowing, becoming less intense, her muscles gradually easing as the sweet tranquillity that follows a passionate sexual experience began to overcome her. She relaxed, leaning back against the wall, panting, watching as Belle slowed her actions, licking the last of the juices from her swollen sex before releasing her thighs and sitting back on her heels, wiping her mouth on her bare arm.

Belle remained where she was, kneeling before her charge in a subservient pose, her head bowed. At last she spoke, continuing to avoid Lia's eyes as if unwilling to allow herself to admit to any intimacy between them.

"Put on my overall."

"What?"

"Don't act so damned dumb; put on the frigging overall. That's an order."

Lia stepped across to where she had discarded the garment. She began pulling it on over her legs. It felt warm and smelt of Belle's body as she pushed her arms into the sleeves. She reached down to the zipper and pulled it up to her neck. She turned to face Belle, who stood watching.

"Right, follow me. And stay close. Remember you're the keeper, I'm the captive." With that she placed her hands behind her head and set off down the path.

Lia hurried along and fell into step behind, watching the swagger of her bare arse as she strode along. They were heading back towards the main compound where they had started from. They were walking down a wide alley, between the old buildings. Suddenly someone appeared, walking towards them, followed by two others.

Lia saw the figure in front of her stiffen. Surely she would turn away, conceal her nudity. The three men were coming closer all the time. They must soon realise that Belle was naked, but still the girl walked brazenly onward, making no attempt to hide or cover herself.

So this was it. This was what Belle wanted. To be in Lia's place, to experience the sensation of being forced to exhibit herself. Perhaps too she felt some of the power over men that Lia had wielded and wanted to try it for herself. Perhaps she felt a need to be dominated. Whatever her motives, she was now acting out the fantasy of her dreams for real, and seemed determined to carry the act to its conclusion.

The men had seen them and were nudging one another, pointing at Belle. Lia closed with her naked captor, watching them warily. The three men moved up side by side, so that they blocked the alley. They were only yards away and from their dress Lia could tell they were truck drivers. Belle walked on until she was only a foot from them, then stopped, her legs apart, her bare sex inviting.

Lia stopped too, her mind racing. What should she do? How would Belle react in a similar situation? At last she spoke. "Out the way, guys. We're in a hurry."

One of them spoke. "You'll have to push past. This alley's a bit narrow."

Lia thought for a moment. Belle had put herself in this situation. It was her problem. "Move on," she ordered.

Without hesitating Belle stepped forward, trying to shove her way between the men. They closed ranks immediately, so that she had to push hard against them. Suddenly one of them grabbed her arms, pinning them behind her. At once the others crowded in, groping her breasts and thrusting their fingers between her legs, probing her sex. Lia watched fascinated as they surrounded her. One of them, the largest of the three, was pinning Belle's wrists together with a single hand, while his other was thrust between her legs from behind, the fingers embedded in her vagina. The second forced her legs apart and was teasing her clitoris, while the third had his rough hands on her breasts, kneading and squeezing them. Lia watched Belle's eyes, ready to bring the scene to a halt if she detected fear or panic. But all the time the girl stood impassively as they caressed her, making no attempt to stop them.

In no time the men had her on the ground, one on each side taking an arm and a leg each while the third knelt between her thighs. Lia watched with excitement as he undid his pants and his erect member sprang into view. She looked closely at Belle's features, but could read nothing in them but uncontrolled lust as the man penetrated her.

The violation of Belle was swift and unceremonious. One after the other the men took her, thrusting hard against her open thighs, mauling her breasts, spurting their seed deep into her vagina. And all the time she writhed and moaned beneath them in the throes of ecstasy. Within less than ten minutes the three were standing over her sprawling body, buttoning their pants and grinning sheepishly at one another. Then they were on their way again leaving the girl panting heavily, her breasts rising and falling as she regained her composure.

Lia pulled her to her feet. She stood before her, red-faced and exhausted in her subservient role, placing her hands behind her head again as Lia brushed the grass and leaves from her hair and back.

"Move on," Lia said at last. Belle turned and, without a word, headed off down the path again, her beautiful arse swaggering provocatively. Lia followed, her mind filled with what she had seen.

They were coming back into a more populated part of the depot and Lia was not surprised when Belle stepped into a doorway and turned to face her, her old dominating manner returned. She took hold of the lapels of the overalls, pulling Lia's face close to hers.

"No one must know what happened here. Do you understand?"

Lia nodded.

"Take off the overall."

Lia was suddenly nervous of being watched, yet aware that the caution was absurd, that the decision as to who should see her unclothed was no longer her own. She obeyed, unzipping the garment to reveal her firm young breasts once more, then stepping out of the lower half.

Belle unexpectedly pulled Lia to her, kissing her lips, their breasts crushed together and Lia's leg forced between Belle's thighs, rubbing against her bare sex, feeling the wetness of the men's sperm on her skin. For a short time the two women stood there, locked in a passionate embrace, their naked young bodies a sharp contrast to the shabby doorway in which they stood.

Chapter 6

The Reception

A banging on the cell door brought Lia awake with a start. She was momentarily uncertain of where she was. The light on the ceiling shone down with a harsh glare, making her screw up her sleep-filled eyes as she tried to get her bearings. Slowly it began to come back to her. The river, the highway, the diner, Belle, the indenture. She found herself blushing with shame as she recalled the events of the previous day.

She looked around. She was lying on a narrow metal bed that hung from a bare, cold brick wall. Next to the bed was a chair, but apart from that the room was empty. An old and rather smelly blanket was all she had in the way of bedclothes. Above where she lay was a small barred window, through which she could just discern the red light of dawn. Three sides of the cell were brick, the fourth an iron grille with bars set vertically about five inches apart. A man was standing on the other side of the grille, by his ragged dress obviously a fellow worker. He was banging a piece of metal against the bars, the clash of the blows ringing round the close walls. When he saw she was awake he stopped.

"Morning!" he shouted. It was not said as a greeting but as a statement of fact.

"What...?" She was still barely awake as she looked at him.

"You the new one? Indenture for sale at the auction?"

"Ye-es."

"It's morning. Time to get up."

Lia tried to raise herself, then realised she couldn't. She looked at her hands. Her wrists were locked in metal shackles attached to the corners of the bed behind her head. An attempt to move her legs confirmed that they were similarly secured.

"I, I can't get up," she said. "I'm chained."

The man grinned. "Chained, eh? They must want to keep you pretty bad. Belle was it?"

"Yes."

The events of the previous evening began to come back to Lia. They had returned to the main centre of the depot and Belle took her into an accommodation block. There she was placed in the charge of a female captive who sat and watched as she bathed and washed her hair. After that she had been given a meal of thick meaty broth that she consumed hungrily at a bare table, alone in an empty room. Then she was led to this cell. Belle had reappeared then, ordering that she be shackled, before the blanket was placed upon her and she was left for the night. She had fallen almost immediately into a deep and dreamless sleep from which she had only awoken at the sound of the crashing of the bar against her cell door.

The man still lingered, gazing at her. She began to feel uneasy. "What do you want?" she said at last. "I can't get up. I told you."

The man did not reply, his eyes fixed on her. Lia shifted uncomfortably, aware that the blanket had slipped in the night, her left side partly exposed, the nipple of that breast barely covered.

"You naked?" the man asked.

Lia reddened and closed her eyes, wishing he would go.

"Hey, I said are you naked? Under that blanket I mean. You got any underwear on?"

"Leave me alone," she replied, her eyes still shut.

"You are, aren't you? You're frigging starkers under there."

"So what if I am?" Lia regretted saying the words immediately, aware that they were virtually an admission.

The man continued, talking more to himself than to her now. "Frigging naked. Just that blanket on her. And chained so tight she can't do nothing about it. This I gotta see."

With that he was gone. She heard his footsteps fading down the corridor, then for a while there was silence.

Lia wondered where he could have gone. Clearly the door to the cell was locked, but still she felt insecure. After all, she was unable to move from the bed.

She didn't have long to wait. Within less than two minutes she heard the sound of footsteps returning. And she could hear whispered voices, and gathered he was not alone. Sure enough, when he appeared he had three others with him, all clearly workers by their dress. They crowded up to the bars, gazing in at her.

"See. She's frigging starkers under there."

"Ah, you can't tell. Might be wearing knickers."

"I tell you she's not got a bloody stitch. Frigging bitch virtually admitted it when I asked."

"Try again."

"What you wearing, darling? Come on, we can keep a secret."

Lia lay where she was, not answering.

"Listen darling," his voice was becoming more menacing, "you may be behind bars but we can still make you pretty uncomfortable. Now answer. What are you wearing?"

Lia's throat was dry; she could barely speak. "Nothing," she said at last.

"See? I told you. You heard her."

"Well let's have a look then. Where's the pole?"

Lia turned to look at them, her eyes wide. Her heart sank as she saw what they were doing. The one who had woken her was wielding a long wooden pole with a metal hook on the end, like they had used in the hostel to open the high windows in the public rooms. She watched anxiously as he extended it through the bars towards her.

The pole was thick and clearly heavy and proving quite a handful for its manipulator. For a while it swayed crazily about in the air, threatening to crash to the floor as he tried to guide it. At last, however, he managed to bring it down so that the hook rested on the bed beside her. Gingerly he eased it forward, under the blanket until she felt the cold metal against her side. Then he began to twist it slowly so that the hook caught in the thin covering.

He began to withdraw the pole. As he did so it dragged the blanket from her upper body. For a moment it had the opposite of the desired effect, pulling the material over the partially exposed breast. Then as he continued to ease it out it slowly exposed her right breast, the hem catching momentarily on her nipple before falling free and rising over the swell of her left. Then it fell away, uncovering her almost to the waist. At the same time the hook slipped from the edge of the bed, clattering to the floor under the weight of the blanket. The man hauled it back in. Lia's breasts were now fully exposed, their young firmness making them stand proudly, despite her supine position, the nipples pointing up towards the ceiling. The men jostled for a view.

"Look at those tits!"

"What a pair of beauties!"

"Like having those nipples sucked, do you love?"

"Don't stop now, let's see the rest!"

Lia watched with apprehension as the pole began reaching out to where she lay again, the metal hook gleaming under the harsh light. Slowly it moved closer until once again the tip was resting on the bed and burrowing beneath her blanket, probing until she could feel it against her hip. Then it began to turn slowly and deliberately, gathering the material round itself, dragging it from her defenceless body. It was pulling up from below this time so that her right foot was exposed, the hem of the material creeping up her leg so that first her knee, then her thighs were bared.

"That's it, you've got it now," said one of the watchers impatiently. "Give it a good pull and let's see what she's got."

The pole gave one last twist, then the man pulled it hard back through the bars. The blanket went too and with it the last vestiges of Lia's modesty. She was left exposed under the harsh light, spread-eagled on the bed, her pink cleft open to their lustful gaze.

"There it is boys!"

"Yeah, look at that, frigging starkers. And proud of it too, by the look of her."

"Fancy a quick fuck, darling? You look as though you would."

"I reckon she's had a few cocks up her in her time."

The crude comments continued as the shackled girl lay unable to move. The crowd was growing as news spread about the block. Some of the onlookers were young women, fighting their way through, as anxious as the men for a look at her. Lia lay like some zoo exhibition, watching the crowd nervously. She thanked her stars that the door was locked, for she had few doubts what would happen if any of them could have reached her.

As the crowd grew so the noise grew with it, the shouts and comments ringing down the hallway. Lia wondered how long it would be before someone in authority came. She tried to blot out the noise of the other captives from her mind, but was constantly reminded of her predicament by their remarks. And in a strange way she found herself turned on by the things being said. She wondered how she would feel if they could get at her, and blushed at the thought.

"What's going on here?"

She recognised the voice as Belle's. She had never thought she would be so pleased to see her!

There was a slight commotion, then the crowd parted to allow Belle through. She gazed through the bars at the naked girl. "You at it again?" she asked harshly. "I can't turn my back without finding you in the centre of trouble. Now come on you lot. Clear out of here. Haven't you ever seen a naked woman before?"

With much muttering and complaining the group dispersed, leaving Belle alone in the corridor. Lia was impressed with her power over the other workers. She noticed for the first time that Belle's overall was a different colour from the rest. It was grey, where all the others wore a dirty brown. Clearly this was a badge of her privilege.

Belle remained at the door for a short time, gazing down at Lia. "I can see you're going to be more trouble than you're worth," she said. "The sooner we find something useful for you to do, the better." Then she was gone, leaving Lia to gaze at the harsh light in the ceiling and ponder her fate.

Time passed, and the sounds from the accommodation block became less and less. Lia guessed the others were leaving for their daily task. Still she was left, spread across the iron bed, dwelling on her predicament. Occasionally a shabby figure would pass the cell and she guessed that these were indentured cleaners and other domestics, carrying out their daily chores. She remained quiet and still when they passed, so that none of them noticed that the cell was still occupied, leaving her to her thoughts.

All at once she heard the sound of a key being turned in a lock. She looked fearfully, disturbed by this sudden breach of her security. A girl stood in the doorway. Lia recognised her as the one who had attended her the previous evening. She was small and blonde, her eyes bright blue, her long hair so fair it was almost white. Her overall fitted tightly, revealing the smooth curves of her body, her backside round and tight. Lia tried to engage her in conversation the night before, but had simply been shushed into silence. She had gathered the girl's name was Eva from the way Belle addressed her, but nothing more. Now the girl stood over her, holding in her hand a bowl of some kind of steaming broth.

She set the bowl on the table and began silently removing the shackles. Lia's arms were stiff with being stretched above her head all night and she rubbed them tenderly, hugging her hands to her breasts as the girl released her legs. Once free she got to her feet, stretching luxuriously, massaging the sore muscles in her arms and legs.

Eva, still silent, indicated the bowl on the table, then was gone, locking the cell door behind her, leaving Lia alone once again. She continued standing, wind-milling her arms as best she could in the tight space, feeling her muscles loosen after the cramped night. She spotted her blanket, still lying on the floor where the men had dropped it, picked it up and wrapped it round herself, grateful for something to cover her nakedness. Then she sat down on the edge of the bed, eating the hot thick gruel. It warmed her and filled her so that by the time she placed the bowl down she was feeling more able to face the day.

The girl Eva returned, this time leaving a bowl of water and some soap. Lia discarded the blanket and began her ablutions. The water was cold but she didn't care, standing up in the bowl and letting the water wash down her body, her skin tingling with its chill.

There was no towel so she wrapped the blanket around herself once again, then sat on the bed, waiting.

Eva returned shortly afterwards to remove the water. Then she held her hands out, indicating the blanket. Lia hesitated, then reluctantly unwrapped it, handing it to the girl who dropped her eyes and hurried from the cell. Less than a minute later she was back, producing a comb from her overalls. She sat Lia on the bed, then settled behind and began running the comb through Lia's hair.

Lia began to feel an affection for the silent little companion who seemed to wait upon her so willingly. She leaned back against her, the motion of the comb soothing. They remained thus for some time, Lia with her eyes closed while the girl ran the comb down through her long shining hair, smoothing it with her hands.

Eva dropped the comb and began massaging Lia's shoulders, her hands manipulating the muscles expertly, rubbing up and down her neck, caressing her spine, making Lia sigh aloud with the sensation, lolling her head back so that their cheeks touched. For a while Lia was perfectly happy, the caresses of her young companion calming her mind and body, drifting her into a trancelike state, oblivious to her surroundings.

At last the girl ceased the massage, resting her hands on Lia's shoulders so she was brought gently back into consciousness. She looked up into the face of the young girl and smiled, then she reached up for Eva's cheek, gently pulling the girl's face to her own. For a moment Eva resisted, then she allowing Lia to kiss her on the mouth, keeping her lips closed at first, but then letting Lia's tongue penetrate, meeting it with her own in a long and passionate embrace. They stayed locked together for long seconds, their tongues probing one another, their eyes closed, allowing the kiss to linger, savouring the moment.

It was Eva who finally broke the spell, pulling gently back from Lia's face, releasing the contact. She untwined Lia's hands from her and stood up, leaving Lia staring up at her from the bed. Still unsmiling she took Lia's hands in hers, raising her to her feet, emphasising her own petite form. She barely came up to Lia's chin when standing.

She motioned Lia to turn around, then Lia felt the cold metal of a pair of handcuffs close over her wrists. Eva opened the door and led her out into the corridor.

They followed a maze of passages, then ascended some stairs and passed along more hallways so that Lia soon lost track of where she was. At last they arrived at a door where the girl paused. She turned to face Lia, then glancing about to ensure they were unseen, reached up and pulled Lia's face down, kissing her briefly. She ran her hands down over Lia's breasts, kissing her gently on each nipple. Then she opened the door, gestured Lia to enter, turned without a word and was gone back down the corridor. Lia gazed after her, longing to embrace her again.

"Come in!" The harsh voice came through the open door, jolting Lia back to reality. She stepped through the entrance, her confidence deserting her along with her little friend.

Inside was a long room, the walls whitewashed, the floor bare. Opposite the door was a desk and chair, where sat a severe looking woman, and beyond stood a ragged queue of men and women outside another door.

"Come here," the woman ordered. In front of her was a sign: *Miss Gorman*. She wore thick-rimmed glasses, her hair neatly pinned into a bob, her face thin and devoid of make-up. She regarded Lia with undisguised disgust.

"How dare you come in here like that?" she said indignantly. "Have you no shame?"

Lia shrank under her gaze, wishing her hands were not pinned so that she could cover herself. "I've got no clothes," she said.

The woman snorted and muttered something about loose women. "Who sent you?" she demanded.

"I, I was brought. I don't know why."

"Where do you work?"

"I don't know."

"You don't know? Of course you know. Don't be impertinent."

"I only arrived yesterday."

The woman consulted a book, keeping Lia waiting for some time as she scanned its pages. "Arrived yesterday, you say? Well I've no record here. What did they say?"

"I've been indentured, to be sold at the auction. The man who brought me in was called Perce. Then I went to see Vargo."

The sound of Vargo's name had the same magic effect on the woman as it had on the truckers the previous day. "Vargo, you say? You actually saw him?"

"Yes."

"Well there's no excuse for laxity. I should have been informed." She glanced up and down Lia's body once again. "You'd better wait in the queue, though what they'll make of you in that state I shudder to think. It's perfectly disgusting."

Lia made her way to where the queue stood. All eyes were upon her and she found herself blushing. She turned and faced the wall in a vain attempt to avoid their gazes.

She was still in the same position half an hour later. The queue had not moved, though more had joined behind. All stood silently, the only sound the scratching of the woman's pen as she scribbled in the ledger. Lia wondered what they were waiting for. She wished she had some clothes, something to cover herself, to allow her to blend into the crowd. As it was, in these dreary, officious surroundings she felt badly out of place.

Suddenly the silence was broken by the harsh sound of a buzzer on the desk. Lia felt the tension in the room rise as the woman got to her feet. She pushed past the motley queue to the door, where she turned to face them.

"Straighten up that line," she commanded. "Come on now. Stand upright, face the front."

The men and women shuffled into line and waited patiently while the woman unlocked the door.

As they reached the doorway Lia could see the others breaking off to right and left. The man in front of her went to the left, and then it was her turn. She stopped, her mind a turmoil of indecision, but the momentum from behind was too great and she felt a shove at her back. She staggered forward, her manacled hands useless to steady her, and fell to the floor with a crash. She lay there for a moment, shocked and dazed, unable to get to her feet, while behind her the rest of the workers took their places in the two ranks.

Suddenly she became aware of a black leather boot by her face. She craned her head around, looking up to see a Biker standing over her. He was a thin, cruel looking man with small black eyes and a knife scar down his left cheek. He was looking down at her as she lay sprawled on the floor, his eyebrows raised in a quizzical manner.

For what seemed like an age the tableau was frozen; Lia lying where she had fallen, the Biker standing over her, the two ranks behind still and silent and the woman supervisor standing at the door. Then, as if suddenly awoken the woman sprang into life. She hurried across, tut-tutting, then grabbed Lia's arm and hauled her to her feet.

Lia stood confused, wondering which way she should go, anxious to not be the centre of attention. She looked about uncertainly.

"Stand still!" the woman barked. Lia froze, standing erect, head up in an instinctive reaction to the order.

"I'm sorry, Flynn." The woman handed a clipboard to the Biker. "This one's been nothing but trouble. Arrived last night apparently. Vargo has seen her, but she's not on my list. For auction, apparently, and a good thing too. It's an affront to decency going about like that, flaunting herself."

The man took the clipboard from her. "It's OK," he said dismissively, "I'm expecting her." He waved a hand and the woman retreated from the room, closing the door.

Everyone was silent once again, the only sound the creaking of the man's boots as he turned and walked to a bare table.

"Come here." He beckoned and Lia shuffled forward, stopping just in front of him.

"So you're the new one. I've been hearing a few stories about you." Lia blushed, only too aware of the sort of stories Perce and his companions would have been telling.

The man stood aside. "Sit on the table," he said. Lia obeyed, turning again to face the others. "Now lie back."

Lia lay back against the hard wood, her arms trapped awkwardly beneath her.

"Open your legs."

Slowly, reluctantly, Lia spread her legs apart. She lifted her head and gazed between her breasts. All eyes were upon her as she laid her sex open to their gaze.

Flynn removed the black leather gauntlet he wore on his right hand. He reached out and stroked her inner thigh, running his hand across the skin until his thumb rested against her sex lips. He ran it gently up and down, applying light pressure on her love bud. Immediately Lia felt her juices start to flow as a spark of lust kindled inside her. He went on rubbing, circling her clitoris, teasing it into life, making her moan slightly with the sensation. He slid his index finger into her vagina, turning his hand palm-up and forcing it inside

74

her, almost lifting her hips from the table. Lia gasped with the sensation, her breasts heaving as she fought for breathe, a sob breaking involuntarily from her lips.

He removed his hand, wiping his finger on a cloth he took from his pocket. "They were right," he murmured. "You are a sexy little thing."

He left Lia where she was on the table as he addressed the other prisoners. She lay, ashamed of her wilfulness, especially that it had been witnessed by so many fellow captives. She wished he would let her get up, at least close her legs, hide the wetness she knew must be visible to all.

Flynn walked down the two ranks of workers, checking names from the clipboard. They stood silent, only answering with a brief "sir" when their names were mentioned.

As each one responded he read back from the clipboard. For those awaiting punishment it was "fined" or "a week's hard labour" and so on. For the redeployed it was "kitchens, gardens, maintenance". Finally he returned to Lia. He consulted his clipboard once more.

"Hm... apparently you're for the stores. That should keep you busy."

Flynn left her lying there while the others were dispatched to their places of work. After they had all gone he looked at her. He grasped her chin, gazing down into her eyes while his other hand slid down and began probing her sex lips, causing another sharp intake of breath.

"I'm almost tempted to fuck you, little one," he murmured, "and judging by the wetness of your sex hole you'd enjoy it." He thrust two fingers deep inside her, feeling her muscles contract around them with a rhythmic pulsation that divulged her latent passion, her hips gyrating slightly as he moved his fingers back and forth. "But there's work to be done, and you're supposed to be in the stores."

He stood for a minute longer, frigging her, enjoying the sight of her uncontrolled lust rising within, and of the warm moisture that seeped from her vagina, wetting the insides of her thighs. Then he withdrew, leaving her panting, and pressed a button on the desk.

Almost at once a door opened; a different one that Lia had not noticed before. A figure entered. Lia's heart jumped as she saw Eva. Little Eva, her waitress and groom, whom she had been kissing so sweetly just a short time before. What must she think now as she stood staring at Lia, lying so that her body was so blatantly spread, her sex open and glistening with the moisture of arousal? Lia closed her eyes in shame.

The girl showed no emotion, but simply stood submissive, awaiting her orders.

"She's to work in stores." Flynn didn't bother even to look up.

Eva motioned for Lia to rise from the table, then again put on the cuffs, pinning her hands behind her back. Then she moved to the door and they went out into the corridor, Lia glad to get away from the wretched room.

Another walk through numerous corridors followed, the girl guiding her through the ups and downs until Lia recognised they were approaching the entrance hall where she had been brought in the day before. As they came closer the sound of voices reached them, and Lia was able to make out a group of figures, who turned to face them. The bulk of Vargo was unmistakable, and Lia's heart sank as she heard him call out.

"You! Come here!"

They hurried across to where the men stood, Eva shoving Lia forward nervously, clearly tense in the presence of Vargo. The two of them stood, Eva slightly behind and to the side, as Vargo's penetrating gaze surveyed Lia.

"Gentlemen, this little item is going up for auction at the sale, a five year indenture, though I don't think she's quite the sort of thing you're looking for. More the sort of merchandise Helda will be after. Have a look."

He turned to Eva. "Turn her round and bend her over." Eva didn't hesitate. She took Lia by the shoulders and turned her. Then she pressed down, so that Lia was forced to bend, staggering to keep her feet as she was forced over. As she adopted the uncomfortable posture, her legs spread wide so that she was staring between them, her tethered hands forced up her back so that they pointed to the ceiling, she was aware of how tight her buttocks were, the cheeks forced apart so that her anus and sex were cruelly revealed.

She remained as she had been placed, her spine bent almost double. Between her legs she could see the jeans of the men as they gathered round. Vargo's voice was distinctive.

"See that slit? Just feel it. Feel how wet she is."

Lia felt a hand run over her buttocks, sliding down the crack and caressing the lips of her sex. She felt her vagina penetrated by a finger, then a second, then a third.

"I see what you mean, Vargo. Very nice. Should fetch a good price."

The fingers worked back and forth for a short time, then just as suddenly withdrew.

"Stand up."

She straightened and turned, her face flushed with shame. What must Eva think of her now? One of the Bikers was holding up his wet fingers.

"Lick them," Vargo ordered.

Lia opened her mouth, allowing the man to place his fingers inside. They tasted salty and smelt of woman.

"Should make a few men very happy," said Vargo.

He turned to the others. Two of them were grinning at the remark, but the third was looking at Lia altogether differently. Then her heart gave a sudden jolt. It was him! The man in the diner. The beautiful blond with the soft blue eyes. And she had been behaving so shamelessly in front of him! She wanted to turn away, but couldn't resist those eyes. For a second she was captivated by their compassion. There seemed a strange intimacy between him and her, as if they were old friends - lovers, even. She felt deeply embarrassed, lowering her head, unable to sustain his gaze.

She realised Vargo was still talking, and hoped he hadn't addressed any orders to her since she had heard nothing. She concentrated on his voice.

"...Found her wandering about on the highway stark naked, trying to hitch a ride. Decided she'd make a good price and I'm inclined to agree. She's got the right temperament; let one of those Defence Force bastards fuck her in the diner without a word of complaint."

The two other Bikers laughed heartily. Vargo turned to the blond man. "What's the matter, Thorkil, you seem to be preoccupied by the item. Want her, do you?"

Lia was shocked, not by the remark, the casual way in which her body was being offered, but by the warm feeling that engulfed her at Vargo's casual words; her stomach flipped and the muscles of her sex contracted involuntarily at them. Thorkil! The name seemed to speak to her of Nordic gods. Thorkil! It seemed to go round and round in her mind like an echo. She looked at him again, almost wishing he would accept, would allow her to be bound hand and foot and then take her at his will. But he smiled gently and shook his head.

"We're here to see what you're offering in the way of manpower," he said, the gentle authority in his voice reminding Lia of how he had rescued her from the mob in the diner.

"Right," said Vargo, appearing to lose interest in her. "Time we were getting on."

They moved off, talking animatedly. The two girls waited until they were out of sight, then Eva nudged Lia and indicated the door, just as a shout came from the other side of the hall.

"Wait!"

It was Belle. She had been sitting at the desk all along, watching the performance. She walked across to them. "If she's working in the stores she needs a lab coat. I'll take her."

Eva dropped her eyes and retreated, leaving Lia once more in the control of the mysterious girl.

Once she was gone Belle turned to Lia. "Come on," she said. "After all, we can't have you walking around completely naked all the time."

Lia thought a smile crossed the girl's face, but she wasn't sure. "This way." Belle indicated a door leading off the hallway, so with a full heart, her mind in a whirl, Lia turned and followed.

Chapter 7

The Stores

The idea that she was to get a lab coat, something at least to cover her body, had seemed to Lia a godsend when Belle suggested it. Now, however, leaving the clothing shop, she was less sure. She had been taken there by Belle and unshackled while the slaves in the shop, which handled all the depot's working clothing, gathered to watch. Then the supervisor made a great show of measuring her, lingering long over her breasts and inside leg, managing to run his hands over most of her body while his assistant looked on sniggering. He produced a coat but Belle rejected it, selecting instead one that was obviously far too small.

Lia felt self-concious as she struggled into the garment. It was made of a thin white nylon that took on the hue of her skin when pressed close. She managed to fasten the two buttons at the waist but was unable to do up the buttons above, so that her breasts bulged out of the opening, nipples barely covered by the straining material. And the minimal length of the coat meant the lower swell of her buttocks were visible below the hem.

As they stepped out of the shop into the morning sunshine Lia felt very uncomfortable indeed. The tight material restricted her legs so that her walk was reduced to tiny steps, and with her arms pinned behind her she was unable to control her breasts, which jutted conspicuously from the open coat as the fabric was pulled open, uncovering her cleavage completely.

The stores was a long brick built structure, at one end of which was a pair of tall doors through which vehicles were constantly passing, carrying spare parts for the many trucks under repair in the depot. Belle led her in through a side door and took her into a small empty office, where she was ordered to wait.

Belle was gone for about ten minutes, and returned with a woman wearing the familiar grey overall of the privileged ones. In contrast to Belle the woman was much older, fat with unkempt hair and calloused hands. She stopped short when she caught sight of Lia, and gave a grunt of surprise.

"Was that the best the clothes shop could do?"

Belle grinned. "I thought it was rather fetching."

The fat woman laughed heartily, slapping her thigh. "I don't know what the rest of the workforce will make of it," she said. "Still, it's not for long, is it? I hear she's destined for a job that will suit her more obvious talents."

It was Belle's turn to laugh. "Well I'm sure you can put her to good use in the meantime. I've got to get back to work."

She undid Lia's shackles, placing them in the pocket of her overall. She ran her hand over the girl's breasts. "Now, you make yourself useful here and don't go giving Olga any trouble." Then she turned and was gone.

Lia stood, awaiting orders from her new mistress. She knew this was an opportunity for her, that if she worked well she might be able to gain some of the privileges the others enjoyed. She was anxious to please.

"You ever worked a computer terminal?"

The question surprised her. She nodded. "Yes." The clothing factory where she had worked had dozens of terminals and she became adept at using them very quickly.

"Well follow me then, and cover up your bloody tits." Lia scurried after the woman, struggling to drag the coat over her breasts as she went.

They were going deeper into the building and she could hear the sound of industry all around. They reached a door marked SUPPLY ROOM 25, and underneath it PARTS 13.000 to 19.000.

Olga produced a card which she wiped down a reader on the door. A tone sounded for a few seconds, then the door swung open and they stepped inside, into a brightly-lit room lined on both sides with shelving, each shelf labelled and stocked with some kind of spare parts. There were thousands of the shelves, layer after layer each with its own unique number and contents. At the far end of the room she caught the green flicker of a computer screen and beyond it some piece of machinery was making a quiet whirring sound. There was a man there, a youngster of about twenty-five, tall and broad-shouldered. He was standing at the computer terminal, and turned to face them as they approached.

"OK Stefan," the woman said as they approached, "we've found someone to take over in here. Show her the ropes as quick as you can. I need you in the loading bay in fifteen minutes." With that she turned and was gone.

"Right," said the man, "come over here and I'll show you what to do. Come on now, you heard what Olga said."

Lia hastened to him, moving as fast as the restrictive garment would allow, seeing his eyes widen with surprise.

"What the hell are you wearing?"

She faltered in her steps, reddening. "They gave it to me in the clothes shop."

"Don't you have anything to wear underneath?" He shook his head, whistling softly, his eyes roving over her shapely form. She wondered what she must look like, her breasts almost bursting out, her slim waist tightly outlined, her hips barely covered, the dark shadow of her pubic hair showing through the semi-transparent material. He continued to study her for some time while she waited, wishing he would get on with explaining the job to her. Then the computer screen bleeped and shook him from his thoughts.

"Right. A request for parts has come through. Here's the serial number." He pointed to the screen. "All the parts are laid out in order on the shelves. You simply find the right one, read the barcode into the computer and put it on the belt. Watch."

She watched him read the number from the screen, then walk down the rows to find what was wanted. Once he found it he ran a light pen over the label and placed it on a conveyor belt. Within seconds the object had disappeared from view through a hole in the wall.

The computer bleeped again. "Your turn," he said.

Lia imitated his actions, easily finding the part in the ordered rows of shelves, reading the barcode and placing it on the belt.

"That's fine," he said. "Just one more thing. If it's on the top shelf you have to slide the ladder along. Just try that now."

Lia grasped the ladder, which ran on oiled rails, and pushed it along.

"Good, now climb up and get a part from the top shelf." She climbed agilely up the ladder, but it wasn't till she was reaching for the part that she realised his motive. Up there on the ladder in the short coat she was giving him a perfect view of her sex. She blushed deeply, hurrying down as fast as she was able.

He took her through the task twice more, forcing her to climb the ladder whether it was necessary or not, but at last he appeared satisfied.

"OK," he said, "I'll leave you to it. Just make sure you're quick. You've got two minutes from when the order first comes through. Fifteen minutes break at one o'clock for lunch. I'll see to it that someone brings you something. Might even do it myself." He winked and was gone.

Lia relaxed, glad to be left alone at last, away from the gaze of other people. She stretched, allowing her breasts to spring free of the coat, no longer concerned about how she looked.

The computer sounded its tone and she was galvanised into activity, retrieving the part and sending it on its way in no time. This was easy. If only it wasn't for the stupid coat impeding her movements. Why not take it off? After all, she was alone. She checked the room. At the far end, behind the computer terminal, there was a small alcove that was concealed from the door. All she needed to do if she heard anyone coming was to dash in there and she would be able to slip it back on unseen. She glanced about guiltily, then peeled it off.

The computer bleeped again and she set about her work, glad to be occupied and glad to be free of the restrictions of the ridiculous coat.

For the rest of the morning she went about her duties conscientiously, running up and down the room, climbing the ladder agilely, delivering the goods to the conveyor belt swiftly and efficiently. So it was a surprise when she heard the sound of the tone caused by the card being swiped at her door, so much so that she barely had time to dash into her little alcove and struggle into the coat before Stefan reached the terminal.

"What are you doing round there?"

Lia, momentarily flustered by his sudden and unexpected arrival, reddened. "N-nothing."

He grinned, and she sensed he was playing with her. "Seems a funny place to do nothing," he said. "Here." He held out a paper bag.

Lia opened it. Inside was a thick sandwich containing some sort of cheese, an apple and a bottle of water. She sat at the terminal eating while he stood watching her. When she had finished he took the empty bag from her. "See you at afternoon break," he said, winking at her as he had before. Then he was gone.

Lia slipped into the corner again and stripped off the coat. She placed it carefully in the same place as before and went back to work.

The afternoon passed swiftly, the insistent bleep of the computer keeping her constantly busy, though at all times she kept one ear open for the return of Stefan. Sure enough, mid-afternoon, she heard footsteps outside the door. Immediately she dashed for her hiding place, flattening herself against the wall and reaching for the coat.

It wasn't there!

She panicked, staring around in disbelief. Where on earth was it? She had definitely left it there. The door had opened and she could hear footsteps coming closer. What was she to do? She bitterly regretted removing the coat now. She pressed herself hard against the wall, trying not to breathe.

"Where are you?" It was Stefan.

"Just here. It's OK, leave the stuff." She tried to keep the panic from her voice.

"What are you doing round there?"

"Nothing," she said, regretting the futility of the remark.

"That's what you said at lunchtime."

Lia, unable to think of a reply, remained where she was, wishing he would go. Then her heart sank as she heard him coming closer. Instinctively she covered her breasts and sex with her hands as he came round the corner.

"There you are," he said. "I've brought you something to eat." He held out the bag.

Lia stared at him for a moment, hesitating. He shook the bag, offering it to her. She was in a quandary, not wishing to move her hands from their protective position, but obliged to react to his gesture. Taking a deep breath she uncovered her breasts and reached for the bag. He snatched it back, leaving her hand waving in mid-air.

"You're naked!" he said in mock surprise. "Where's your uniform?"

"I don't know," she said, struggling to cover her breasts again.

"That's a punishable offence, losing your uniform. I'll have to report it."

"No, please..."

"I have to report it. I have to make sure you're punished, you see."

"Couldn't you help me find it?" Lia realised she was playing his game, but the thought of that dreadful woman was too much.

"It depends. You still need to be punished."

Lia sensed what he wanted. "Couldn't you punish me?" she said quietly. She let her arms dangle by her sides, allowing him to see her nakedness unimpeded.

He leered. "Now there's a good idea." He sat on a chair and beckoned to her. "I think a good spanking is required," he said. "Over my knee."

Lia couldn't believe it. He wanted to spank her like some naughty schoolgirl! She hadn't been spanked since she was a child, and even then never naked. She stared at him.

"Over my knee," he repeated.

Lia struggled to think of something to say, something to prevent the humiliation he proposed to inflict upon her, but it seemed she had no choice. Slowly, reluctantly she bent over him as he sat, so that her feet and hands touched the floor on either side of the chair, her bare buttocks stretched taut over his lap. He placed a hand on her back, pushing her further down while his other hand forced her to open her legs.

She felt his hand on her backside, caressing the round cheeks of her arse and sliding down between her thighs. His fingers began to stray over her sex lips, sliding down the furrow until they brushed her love bud, teasing it gently into life. She felt it swell under his touch, responding to his caresses in a manner completely beyond her own control. His fingers worked it back and forth while his thumb penetrated her open vagina, delving deep inside her, his slight movements controlling the tide of her lust, playing her tense body, causing her to moan involuntarily.

Smack! He brought the flat of his hand down hard on her left cheek so that she squealed with surprise and pain.

Smack! This time it was her right cheek, the blow catching her just above the tops of her legs. Then his fingers resumed their caresses, probing deep inside her, making her thrust her bottom back, tightening her nether globes.

Smack! Unable to resist the improved target he brought his hand down again. She was whimpering, partly with the shame and pain of the punishment, partly with the passion he was generating as his fingers again probed her wet vagina.

Smack! Smack! Smack!

The punishment continued. Lia's arse was red with the imprints of his hand as she writhed with the alternate pleasure and pain he was meting out to her. She had shifted her position slightly so that the motion was causing her to rub her clitoris against the coarse material of his overall, making her grunt with arousal.

Smack! Smack!

The beating seemed to be going on forever. The cheeks of her backside were quivering under the blows, and the more he struck her the wetter her sex became, so that her cheeks glistened with her own juices. Her motions were becoming more insistent, thrusting herself unashamedly against him.

Smack! Smack!

The computer bleeped. For a moment he held her where she was, still driving her love bud urgently against his knee. Then he shoved her off so that she sprawled on her back at his feet, legs apart, panting with pain and desire. He pushed her aside with his foot. "Come on," he said, "back to work."

82

Lia struggled unsteadily to her feet. She gazed around dazedly. The computer; she stared at the screen, momentarily unable to comprehend its message. Somehow she managed to discern the number. She staggered down the row of shelves, screwing up her tear-stained eyes, trying to find the right one. She grabbed at a part, swiped the barcode on the third attempt and dropped it on the conveyor belt. Then she turned to face Stefan, swaying slightly.

He grinned. "Thought you weren't going to make that in time." He moved close to her, running his hands through her hair before letting them drop onto the firm globes of her breasts. "My, what a hot little thing you are," he said, smiling. "Let's have a look at that arse."

She turned round, bending at his command, her hands resting in the seat of the chair. She felt him touch her red-hot cheeks.

"Good," he said at last. "That ought to be a lesson to you, though we may have to repeat it now and again. No, don't get up just yet, the view from here is so delightful."

She was forced to submit to his prolonged inspection, bent over, her sex and anus openly displayed, until at last they were interrupted again by the insistent bleep of the machine and Lia set about her duties with relief. By the time she finished Stefan had gone, slipping out without her even noticing.

She worked on for the rest of the afternoon undisturbed. She checked the alcove when she had the opportunity and realised the coat had been snatched through a ventilation grille. He had guessed it was there!

The smart in her backside soon reduced to a dull ache, and she was almost her usual self when she heard the tone from the door late in the afternoon. It was Stefan again, accompanied by Eva. Lia was pleased to see her little friend, though embarrassed to be seen by her naked in front of the man.

Stefan handed her the lab coat, which she struggled into. Then he kissed her lightly on the cheek and left. Eva, silent and unsmiling as always, led her back to the accommodation block.

And so Lia's life slipped into a sort of pattern. She had little contact with the other captives apart from meal times in the canteen. There was a social room where they gathered in the evenings and occasionally she would be taken there by Belle, who would make her stand with her by the bar while the others passed comments and surreptitiously felt her up. But generally her only companion was Eva, who continued her wordless service. Every morning she was taken to the stores and inspected by Olga before being set to work. Then Stefan would appear and demand her coat, which she would hand over reluctantly. Once a day he would visit her again, sometimes lunchtimes, sometimes in the afternoon, and the spanking would be repeated.

On the third day she had disgraced herself by having a violent orgasm during the punishment, her juices flowing as she screamed her desire. After that she hung her head, ashamed, determined to keep herself better under control.

It was towards the end of the second week of captivity that things went really wrong. It was mid-afternoon, and she was working hard, aware that the break was approaching and that Stefan, who had not appeared at lunchtime, was soon due to visit. She felt a strange feeling in her stomach as she always did before his arrival; a sort of pent up desire that made her sex moisten as she anticipated another spanking.

She heard footsteps outside the door and the unmistakable sound of the card being swiped. Immediately she took up the position he had taught her to whenever he visited, bent over double, her legs apart, facing away so that the flesh of her arse was pulled tight and open, her sex enchantingly revealed. The door clicked, and she stood waiting to feel his touch on her bottom.

"Well, well, well."

Lia jumped as she recognised Olga's voice. Flustered she stood upright, her hands moving instinctively to cover herself.

"What do you think you're doing?"

Lia's mouth opened but she was unable to frame an answer, overawed by the presence of the woman and of the compromising circumstances in which she had been discovered.

"Answer me. Where is your coat?"

"I, I, Stefan took it."

"Stefan? Why on earth did you give it to him? Are you two up to something?"

"No."

"Come on, he's been screwing you hasn't he? Right here in the stores."

"No." Lia shook her head violently.

"Well what then? Why were you standing like that? Flaunting yourself so provocatively?"

"I... he... he spanks me."

Olga's eyes widened. "My, but you do have strange tastes."

"It's not me, it's him."

"Then why the hell were you standing like that? You looked to me like someone wanting to be spanked." Lia was unable to answer, and hung her head. "Well," said Olga, "we'll have to see about this. Wasting your time during working hours is a serious offence. Meanwhile I've got a job for you. There's a truck in the back lot that needs some spares urgently. You and I are taking them out by hand."

"But the computer..."

"That's not your problem. Here, this is the list." Olga handed Lia a piece of paper with half a dozen numbers on it. She set about collecting the parts from the shelves, wishing she had something to hide her from Olga's penetrating gaze. Soon all the spares were arranged in a row on the workbench.

"Right," said Olga, "pick them up and follow me."

"But my coat..."

"Follow me, I said. Do I have to repeat all my orders?"

84

Her head in a whirl Lia picked up the parts and followed her down the corridor in a direction she had not been before. They turned off down another passage, then Olga opened a door and Lia found herself standing in the open air, behind the stores building. The area was overgrown and neglected, the concrete path cracked, tufts of coarse grass growing up through the gaps. Clearly this was not a route that was used frequently.

Olga strode on, leading Lia down a passage between two buildings. Lia hurried along behind, clutching the bag of spare parts in front of her in a vain attempt to cover herself. She glanced about, fearful of being seen, wishing they could go back indoors.

The path widened and Lia saw they were approaching a large concreted area. She guessed it was a truck park, though scarcely used now and in danger of being taken over by the dense vegetation. There was a single truck parked there, partly concealed by bushes on two sides of it. As they came closer she could make out an arm projecting from an open window in the cab.

Her attention was caught by the shining chrome radiator grille on the front of the vehicle and she stopped short, dumbstruck. She had seen the truck before! And the last time had been on the highway!

Olga walked around the side of the truck to where the window was open. "This the one?" she called up.

"Dunno. Tell her to do what she was doing then."

"Show them," snapped Olga.

Lia stared at her. Surely she couldn't mean what she thought she meant? "What?" she said lamely.

"You heard me. Show them what you were doing."

"I, I can't."

"Show them. Give me that bag."

Lia took a deep breath, then slowly handed the bag, her only protection, to Olga. She stood, hesitant.

"Show them!" Olga's voice took on a dangerous edge.

Lia looked up at the cab. The two men were watching her intently, their eyes roving up and down her body. She thought of the last time they had met, of her brazenness. She remembered her visualisation of the two of them taking her, of how it had excited her so much. She thought again of what might happen, imagined the two of them ravishing her, and she felt the stirring of lust within her. So they wanted to see her stimulate herself? Well, that was one thing she knew she could do. She looked across at Olga, who was waiting with rising impatience. She knew she could delay no longer.

She placed her hands flat on her thighs, then gradually drew them up her body, over her hips, up her stomach until they were cupped under her breasts. She opened and closed them, squeezing her breasts so that they protruded invitingly. She began rubbing, moving her hands further up her breasts to brush the nipples. She pushed upwards, and bending her head, began licking her breasts, first one, then the other, watching the men through lowered lids.

She covered her nipples with saliva, licking round and round them, teasing them with the tip of her tongue, then working the moisture into them with her fingers.

Once her nipples were erect and glistening she leaned forward, shaking her shoulders from side to side, making the firm globes quiver with the motion. She was in a world of her own, lost in her eroticism, the stimulation of her breasts arousing delicious feelings in her groin. She looked up at her audience. All eyes were fixed on her, the grins gone from the men's faces as they saw the raw lust in her.

She continued to work on her breasts; licking, rubbing, caressing, then offering their swollen flesh up to the men in the cab. Between her thighs she felt juices begin to flow, the familiar sensation, the overall desire to be touched down there becoming almost too much.

At last she could prevent herself no longer, opening her legs wide and reaching eagerly for her swollen love bud, the languid caresses of her breasts giving way to urgent stimulation as she slid her fingers into herself, bending her knees to improve access and improve also the view she was giving to the occupants of the truck. She felt her juices run down her hand onto her thighs and imagined the sight of it, the image making her masturbate all the harder. Between her half-lowered eyelids she saw a door of the cab open and a figure descend.

She felt her hand brushed aside from her sex, replaced by the coarse fingers of the lorry driver. He probed between the lips of her vagina, violating her most private place, confident she was in his power. And Lia made no objection to the assault. On the contrary, she let out a gasp of passion and leant back, placing her hands on her hips, thrusting urgently against the hand, her cries becoming louder as she lost control.

His fingers began to probe even deeper as she impaled herself upon them, her sex burning with desire for him. All modesty and decorum deserted her as she indulged herself shamelessly.

Suddenly he took his hand away, leaving her gasping, the lips of her sex convulsing. She whimpered as she felt him withdraw, gazing at him plaintively.

"It's her all right," he said to Olga. He turned back to Lia and gestured at the truck. "Why not get in the cab?"

She nodded, too aroused to trust herself to speak. He stood aside as she made for the cab, anxious to feel his hands on her again. She paused at the foot of the step as her eye caught Olga's. For a moment they stared at each other, then she felt the man's hand probing between her legs from behind, lifting her up to the open door.

As she climbed inside she glanced back, and glimpsed the man passing a banknote to Olga. She was being sold like a common prostitute, all her rights bartered away with a simple transaction. She belonged to the men for the next few minutes, was theirs for the taking.

These thoughts were banished from her mind immediately as she came face to face with the other man in the cab. She was crawling across the seat on all fours, her breasts hanging bare and inviting. He reached for them, but she only had eyes for the bulge at his crotch, her fingers scrabbling to undo his grimy jeans.

She slid her hand into his briefs and felt the hot flesh of his penis as it uncurled, hardening under her touch. She eased it gently from the briefs, fascinated by its animation as it stiffened before her eyes. She ran her fingers up and down its long thick shaft, pulling back the foreskin, her other hand gently kneading his balls. She leant over the fully erect cock and closed her lips about its helmet, tasting his salty manhood, encouraged by his grunt of satisfaction as she went down on him.

She heard the door of the cab slam behind her, and once again felt the driver's hand sliding up her inner thigh. She widened her legs, inviting him to caress her wet sex as she slid her lips over the other man's member, her head bobbing up and down as she sucked him. The fingers found her hole, penetrating deep within her, only the cock filling her mouth preventing her from crying out.

For a time the fingers continued their intimate caresses, sliding in and out in a rhythm that matched that with which she was orally stimulating her other partner. Then she felt something different. The unmistakable sensation of a rigid penis sliding down the crack in her arse, over her anus and down to her sex, nuzzling briefly against her nether lips before pressing against her clitoris, the glans circling around the swollen bud, probing at it then working up and down the wetness that seeped from her. She moaned softly, the sound muffled by the rigid phallus that filled her mouth, pumping back and forth.

The cock positioned itself at the mouth of her sex. She thrust up and back at it, urging it to enter her, to probe deep within, to fill her with its seed. Still it hesitated and she sensed the man was enjoying her frustration, teasing her into a frenzy of desire.

At last he could wait no longer. The sight of the girl, shamelessly naked, sucking the cock of a stranger, her arse in the air, her legs wide apart revealing a wet and willing hole was too much. Lia felt him press his weapon against her opening, harder, harder, so that at last the tip slipped into her sex. She continued to press back at him, wanting him further inside her, anxious to be fucked hard and deep, oblivious to her crude wantonness as she satisfied the two men.

He began to penetrate further, his sturdy organ stretching the walls of her sex as it forced its entry. The sensation was almost more than she could bear, the muscles of her vagina contracting around it, welcoming its intrusion. Still he pushed into her and she thrust back at him, wanting him to fill her with his rampant organ, to possess her totally. At last she felt his groin hard against her backside, the tip of his organ probing to the very limit of her wet love hole.

Then he was pulling back again, beginning to screw her in earnest, the friction of his massive rod raising her to new heights of eroticism. His motions were slow at first, gyrating his hips so that the sensation was heightened. His hands reached round her body, groping for her luscious breasts that hung like some exotic fruit ripe for the picking. He took them in his strong rough hands and began kneading them, his fingers toying expertly with her jutting nipples, sending her into still more heightened throes of delight.

Her body glistened with sweat as she worked her mouth up and down, the slapping of her other partner's balls against her thighs urging her on. She wanted to give herself completely, to fill her mouth and her vagina with their semen. Simultaneously she felt the tension in her two lovers increase and knew she was not far from receiving it. And that was what she desired more than anything; to feel them empty themselves into her willing flesh. Her own orgasm was close too; she was about to reveal the lust within her in the most intimate way, to display unequivocally her own total arousal.

With a barely suppressed gasp the man grasped her hair, forcing his thighs up at her face and she felt the cock between her lips begin to spurt. Warm streams of thick semen filled her mouth as the spasms began in earnest, his thrusts forcing his cock to the back of her throat. She swallowed frantically, trying to let none escape, to take it all, the nodding motions of her head redoubled in an effort to keep the flow coming.

At the same time she sensed the cock in her vagina pulsate and felt the gush of sperm pumping into her as he consummated his pleasure, filling her with his seed, the copious jets splashing against the very limit of her uterus. That was enough to push her over the edge, the feel of his come squirting into her willing sex triggering her orgasm.

All the pent up feelings of the last two weeks, the exposure, the bondage, the beatings, the humiliation, all were unleashed in that orgasm. Lia screamed out loud, the semen escaping from her lips as she abandoned herself to the delight of the twin organs that filled her. She pumped her hips backwards against the ejaculating cock penetrating her sex, milking it for every drop of pleasure it had to offer, intent on her own lustful desires as she rode out her naked passion in the squalid cab of the truck.

Gradually her passions began to subside, the gyrations of her arse to slow as she descended from the heights of her climax. The cock in her mouth ceased its pumping, and she licked its tip greedily, sighing with disappointment as she felt the stiff organ in her vagina begin to withdraw, to pull out of her wet, satiated hole. As it finally emerged she was aware of the thick gobs of semen beginning to trickle down her thigh.

She rolled onto her back, gazing across at the driver, who was busy fastening his trousers. He studied her with contempt, his eyes roving over her exposed body, her breasts glistening with sweat and semen, her legs splayed shamelessly wide, the evidence of his orgasm smeared on her pubic hair and inner thighs. She knew that he saw her as just another harlot, something to be fucked and discarded, merely a receptacle for his lust, but she didn't care. She had just had raw, unbridled sex with a pair of strangers, and the thought of it made her somehow proud. She might be a captive, but the passions she could arouse in others were, if anything, enhanced by her status.

"Get out, slut." The driver shoved open the door to the cab.

She looked down at her ravished body. She was scarcely in a state to be wandering about the depot in broad daylight. She squinted through the windscreen, but there was no sign of Olga. The man grasped her roughly by the arm. He pulled her up and shoved her out the door, so that she had to make a grab for the handrail, stumbling and rolling onto her back as she hit the ground. She looked up at the truck as its engine roared into life and with a grinding of gears it moved off, leaving her lying alone on the ground.

She scarcely had time to ponder her next move, when a shadow fell across her.

"So there you are, you little tart," said Belle. "I've been looking for you."

Chapter 8

The Punishment

Lia wondered how long she would have to stand there in chains before the punishment would begin. Most of all she wished she could cover herself, that her hands were not cuffed behind her. She was in a small room overlooking the main assembly area, in the front of the building where she had first been brought. Through the window she could see a raised platform, on which she knew they were preparing to mete out her punishment.

All the time groups of people, workers, Bikers and truckers alike, were gathering in the square below, and an almost carnival-like atmosphere prevailed as they waited. Now and then the door to the room would open and a group of Bikers or privileged workers would come in to ogle her in her discomfort. Many fondled her breasts or probed her sex, the lone guard who stood beside her apparently unconcerned at these assaults.

Lia, her desires still latent despite her predicament, would moan softly at the caresses knowing that her sex was moist with the stimulations. Even now as she stood there a young Biker was feeling his way up her thighs. She closed her eyes as yet another hand delved into her vagina, the fingers finding her swollen love bud and causing her to jerk her hips violently with arousal.

She thought back over the last few hours, her encounter in the truck, her discovery by Belle. She had been handcuffed then and there and marched to Vargo's office, the evidence of her ravishment still obvious. She had been forced to stand and listen while Belle had described how she had given herself to the two truckers.

Worse was to come though, when she was shown the video tapes. Of course she should have known there would be security cameras in the stores, that she wouldn't have just been left alone to do as she pleased. She blushed red as she thought of the pictures she had been shown. Bad enough were those of her stripping off the coat and carrying out her tasks naked. But the footage of her bent across Stefan's lap, submitting to his spankings had been too much.

The last straw had been the image of her orgasm, her cries clearly audible as she lay across his knee and submitted to him. She knew the pictures had been circulated about the depot, that Stefan and Olga had been making a tidy profit from the truck drivers by selling copies of her abandoned display. That was how the two truckers recognised her, had told Olga the tale of the wanton girl who had appeared on the highway that day, shamelessly exposing her body to them.

She had been tricked. Fooled into believing she had privacy whilst working in the storeroom naked, fooled into thinking that the loss of the coat had been her fault, and fooled into allowing Olga to sell her to the truck drivers. All along, from the first time she had removed her coat, she had been controlled by those who cared not for her welfare. And now she was awaiting her punishment.

When Vargo declared the punishment twenty strokes in public she had been speechless. Twenty strokes! And in front of all those people! She pleaded for mercy but in vain. Belle led her from his office to this cage, where she had been waiting for nearly two hours, enduring the taunts and abuse of those who came in to stare and to grope. But she knew the moment was close.

There was the sound of footsteps outside the room. She craned round and could just discern figures entering. She recognised Perce, Belle and little Eva. She closed her eyes when she saw her friend, aware that she too must have heard what was happening and probably seen the videos.

Perce barked an order and the guard unlocked the cuffs, allowing his hands to stray over her bare breasts and to finger her sex as he did so, making her catch her breath.

Once she was released Perce ordered her to kneel, then signalled to Eva, who held something in her hands. She unwrapped it, revealing what was a sort of vest, made of a stringy yarn woven loosely, more like a net, the holes in it about the size of a penny piece. Eva draped it over Lia's head and pulled it down so that it just reached to below her buttocks. It had the effect of covering her nakedness without really hiding it, her nipples protruding through the holes and the dark triangle of her pubic hair showing a clear contrast with her pale flesh.

She stood up and waited patiently while Eva shackled her wrists behind her again. A leather collar was buckled round her neck, from which ran a chain like a dog's lead.

Lia's heart was beating hard as she descended the stairs into the hallway, following Eva, who held the lead. Behind came Perce and Belle, whispering to one another. The door opened in front of them and Lia's footsteps faltered as she heard the noise of the crowd outside, so that Eva had to give a tug on the chain to make her follow.

Outside there must have been more than three hundred people packing the square, chattering noisily. As Lia appeared in the doorway the noise ceased and the crowd stood silently, watching her. She held her head high and marched behind Eva, a passage opening in the crowd to allow their progress. As she walked she glanced sideways at the faces of her audience. All were intent on her, their eyes feasting on the lithe young body that was scarcely hidden by the vest. Lia felt the hem of the garment rise up over her buttocks as she walked, but was determined not to appear uneasy. She strode on, intent only on the platform that rose up in the middle of the crowd, the place of her punishment.

They reached the foot of the dais and began to ascend the wooden steps, towards the woman who stood at the top awaiting their arrival. At first Lia failed to recognise her, then realised it was Miss Goram. She had let her hair down so that it draped over her shoulders. The prim dress had gone, replaced by a shiny black leather leotard, cut low across the breasts and high up the thighs. Her legs were clad in black fishnet stockings and stiletto heeled boots that reached to above her knees. On her arms she wore long suede gloves that extended almost to her elbows. Lia realised with a start that she was much younger than she had at first thought. She looked magnificent in her leather outfit.

As Lia stepped onto the platform a murmur went up from the crowd. They jostled forward for a better look, those at the front craning their necks for a view of her sex beneath the short garment. Eva led her to the very edge, then removed the collar and cuffs and retreated back down the stairs.

Perce began some sort of announcement, detailing Lia's crimes to the hushed crowd. Lia barely listened as she surveyed the sea of eyes before her. Beyond the crowds a number of windows in the building were open and she was sure the bulk of Vargo filled one of them.

It was all for her. She would not disappoint them. She was eager for it to begin, proud of their stares and their eager lusting.

With a start she realised Perce had reached the end of his homily and was addressing her. She gazed at him uncomprehendingly.

"Take off the vest," he said again.

Lia turned to face the crowd, which was tense now, aware of the command given. She looked out at them, trying to show no fear. She knew this was what they had come to see, and was determined to give them the show they desired. All eyes were fixed upon her as she took a deep breath, grasped the hem of the garment in both hands and pulled it up over her head in a single movement. For a second she stood holding it in front of her, hiding her nakedness. Then, in a gesture of abandonment, she tossed it carelessly into the crowd below, placing her legs apart and standing hands on hips, her magnificent breasts proud and bare, her open vagina thrust forward for all to admire.

A low whistle came from somewhere in the throng below. Then the comments started.

"Look at that!"

"What gorgeous tits. Wobble them about a bit love."

"Look at the way the brazen little slut's flashing her cunt."

"Yeah, I wouldn't mind getting my cock in there."

"She's bloody wet too. I reckon she's turned on."

"What a lovely arse!"

Lia stood proudly erect, glorying in it all. She felt her arm grasped harshly and was turned to face Miss Goram. Across the centre of the dais was a bar, about four inches thick, supported by two upright struts. It was there that Lia was led. She stood against the bar, which was at just the height of her vagina, so that her pubis rubbed against it. Miss Goram took each foot in turn, stretching them out on either side and shackling them to the uprights.

Then she took Lia by the hands and pulled her forward until she was bent double over the bar. Her hands were then shackled to where her feet were attached. The naked girl was completely helpless, her buttocks stretched taut. The crowd manoeuvred for a better look at her so delightfully splayed, her breasts hanging invitingly.

Miss Goram turned and opened a long case that lay at the side of the dais, and for the first time Lia saw the weapon of her punishment. It was a long cane, about the thickness of her index finger. She shuddered as she watched the woman take a few practice swipes, the cane swishing through the air.

Miss Goram positioned herself slightly behind Lia and to one side. Lia felt a gloved hand stroking the taut flesh of her backside, descending to her love hole and running along the outer lips, so that she felt the juices begin to flow within her. Miss Goram stood back, raised her arm high and brought the cane cracking down onto Lia's raised posterior.

Thwack! The blow cut across diagonally, biting deep into the tender flesh, making the girl yelp with pain, her body convulsing with the strength of the strike. The agony of the blow was intense; surely she couldn't be expected to endure twenty?

Thwack! The second blow cut in the other direction, leaving a white mark that rapidly turned red, making a bright cross on her buttocks, as if marking a target.

Thwack! The third blow caught her at the top of the legs and she screamed as it stung her.

Thwack! This time the cane fell right across the middle of its target, making the full round globes quiver with its force.

Thwack! Once again Lia shrieked as the cane cracked across her unprotected skin. The crowd was silent now, intent on the spectacle before them, excited by the combination of eroticism and brutality on display.

Thwack! The blow fell almost exclusively on her right buttock, the tip of the cane snaking around to her hip.

Thwack! Lia was shrieking with the agony and the ecstasy of the beating, her arse on fire from the hail of blows. There was almost nowhere on her rear that hadn't been touched, so the blows were beginning to fall on areas already red and raw, redoubling the pain.

Thwack! The woman's strength showed no sign of abating as she continued, though a small film of perspiration was forming on her forehead. She appeared to be enjoying the task, the sinews in her arms standing out as she put her full force into the punishing strokes.

Thwack! Through the tears that filled her eyes the tortured girl could still make out the sea of faces that watched fascinated as she was disciplined. She clenched her teeth, trying desperately not to let herself go completely before the crowd.

Thwack! The blows kept on falling. That made eleven, Lia thought, trying desperately to keep count in an effort to retain her senses amid the cacophony of pain.

Thwack! Her whole body was responding to the strokes, rocking back and forth despite the bonds that held her down. Her feet rose clear of the ground in a futile effort to break the chains that held her, to allow her to escape the terrible punishment.

Thwack! Lia's naked body glistened with a sheen of sweat as the blows continued. She was gasping animal-like wails with every stroke, still counting in her mind, determined to retain control.

Thwack! Fourteen. All she could think of was how many more to go. Six! Could she stand another six? She gazed up into the face of her punisher, trying to detect a glimmer of mercy. There was none.

Thwack! Fifteen. Five more to go. The tears were streaming from her eyes, her body shaking as the sobs racked her.

Thwack! Sixteen. Her arse was burning all over, the cruel red weals crisscrossing in a crazy pattern, merging into one another, agonisingly painful.

Thwack! Seventeen. Only three to go. Only! Lia felt she would give anything in the world to avoid those last three strokes. She had no idea that such pain could exist. The whole of her being was centred on the source of the agony.

Thwack! Eighteen, making her writhe all the more at the dreadful stinging blow.

Thwack! Nineteen. The sweat was dripping from her onto the floorboards below, a fine spray arising from her with every strike. Miss Goram was drawing back her arm, clearly determined that the final blow would strike as hard, if not harder than the first.

Thwack! The cane came down for the last time with a terrible force. She screamed as it bit into her punished flesh. It felt like barbed wire rather than a cane she'd been beaten with.

Miss Goram stood back, breathing heavily with the exertion, her face wet with perspiration. She ran a hand over the glowing flesh of Lia's backside, making the girl flinch as if she had struck a further blow, then bent and undid the shackles on her victim's wrists and ankles.

For a long time the sobbing girl remained where she was, heedless of the sight her bare red arse made for the onlookers, too drained to care about anything but the pain. Gradually she felt her strength begin to return and. summoning all her power she slowly straightened up, supporting herself on the bar until at last she stood upright again.

Then slowly, gingerly she turned and faced the crowd and, determined to show her will had not been broken she spread her legs, placed her hands on her hips and thrust her sex in the same defiant gesture she had made before the beating, throwing back her head so that the sun shone down onto her tearstained face. A murmur of appreciation came from the crowd.

There was a touch on her shoulder and she turned to see Eva standing behind her. The girl had been crying. Lia took her cheeks in her hands and kissed her lips, managing a smile. Then she stood obediently while the handcuffs and collar were attached. She threw a final glance at Miss Goram, then allowed Eva to lead her off, her gait pained and awkward. They descended the steps and set off for the accommodation block. The crowd parted before them, watching fascinated as the naked girl was led through, her head high.

Chapter 9

The Auction

The next few days were to be Lia's last at the depot. Belle had visited her cell to tell her that the auction would take place the following week and that she was due to be transported out the day before. Eva visited her often, rubbing a sweet smelling ointment onto her and sitting at her feet while she slept, always there if she woke.

She would bathe Lia daily, soaping her lean body, never speaking but transmitting her thoughts by her actions. At night she would remain staring down at her, as if fascinated by her body, the breasts so firm, the sex so prominent.

The days passed quickly. Those passing the cell would linger to stare at the lovely naked captive until they were hurried on by a wave of Eva's hand.

On her last night Eva knelt down and put her mouth close to Lia's ear. "I'm coming with you tomorrow," she whispered.

Lia's heart leapt. It was the first time she had heard the girl speak. Until then she had not been sure Eva was capable of speech. Now this message filled her with anxiety.

"Not to be sold?" she asked.

Eva shook her head, smiling. "As keeper," she said, and was gone, running down the corridor, leaving Lia to ponder the news. She was glad Eva was to come with her. She had grown to love the young girl and had been dreading their separation. Now at least they had a few more days together. She drifted off to sleep with a serene smile on her face.

The next morning there was a scurry of activity throughout the accommodation block. As well as Lia, a number of other indentured workers were to go to auction and the preparations began at an early hour. Lia was woken by Eva at daybreak, bathed and fed, then left to wait in her cell until she was required. At last Eva came to her, handcuffing her and leading her out to the waiting transport. Lia had been half hoping she would have been given clothes for the journey, but clearly this was not to be the case.

They stepped out of the building into the sunlight and Lia saw a pair of open-backed trucks waiting in the parking lot. One was already almost full with indentured workers, nearly all male, chained to rings bolted to the sides and floor of the truck. It was to this one that Eva led her, helping her up onto the platform and shackling her so that she stood at the rear, facing backwards. Lia pondered on the decision to put her there. It would leave her exposed to any other motorists on the road. She suspected that Perce was responsible for placing her there and was not surprised to see him watching as she was chained in place.

She looked about at her fellow passengers. They were a motley crew, mostly in rags, their faces downcast. Two of them she recognised; Olga and Stefan were chained side by side, the grey overalls of privilege replaced by the rags of common workers. So they had not escaped punishment for their part in Lia's downfall, but she found it hard to rejoice in their misfortune. Apart from any other considerations she did not wish to make any enemies, and judging from the way the two of them were glaring at her, they were none too pleased with how things had turned out.

The engine started, throbbing, rattling and vibrating. She looked about for Eva but couldn't see her. She guessed she would be following behind. There was a grinding of gears and the truck began to move. Lia clung to the bar that spanned the tailgate. They reached the gate and the truck stopped while its cargo was checked, the gateman ticking off each captive on a clipboard, lingering in front of her for a good look. Then they were out on the open road and heading for the auction, the engine roaring as they sped along.

The journey was a long one, the truck rumbling down the highway for some hours. Lia sat, her feet dangling over the tailboard, enjoying the fresh air and the scenery. She tried to follow where they were but soon lost track among the sameness of the highways. Occasionally she would see a road sign, but the names meant nothing to her. The others sat mainly in silence, but Lia didn't care. She was happy with her own thoughts, and eventually, despite the roar of the engine and the bumping motion, she fell asleep.

She was woken by the sensation that the vehicle was slowing. She opened her eyes and gazed blearily about. They were indeed slowing. The truck swung to the left and they were off the main road and heading up a dirt track. It was rough and the truck bounced about, so they were forced to hang on tight. Lia clung to the bar that ran across the tailboard as they lurched along into some woods. They went on for some miles, the forest becoming denser as they progressed. As they penetrated deeper they passed the occasional group of Bikers, clearly there to police the road and to keep out the unwanted.

At last the truck pulled into a vast clearing. The area was a hive of activity. All about there were tents, surrounded by bikes. In the centre was an arena with a large marquee behind. One area had been set aside for trucks to park and already more than a dozen had pulled up there, all like theirs with open backs and anchor points for shackles. The truck lurched across the grass and came to a halt beside them.

The sudden silence was like music to Lia after the clamour of the motor. She sat patiently with the others, awaiting the next move.

Two Bikers emerged from the front of the truck and were joined by two captives in grey overalls, who had evidently been awaiting their arrival. One of the Bikers came round and stood by the tailgate.

"Right you lot," he shouted, "you're all here for your indentures to be sold. Now I don't want you getting any ideas about escaping just because you're out of the depot, so we'll be taking a few precautions. Just wait your turn now."

The men in overalls vaulted up onto the truck and began releasing them one by one. Lia was one of the first, jumping lightly to the ground in front of the first Biker, and they were marched off to their campsite.

Lia realised the clearing was divided into a number of separate campsites, one for each Biker group, of which there were many. Lia calculated that at least thirty separate sites had been set up, each one flying its own distinctive pennant. The Biker gangs had long since stopped the wars that had so bloodily punctuated the early years of their existence, and now lived in peaceful, if slightly strained, harmony, each with its own territory and its own share of the trucking operations.

The indenture auctions, held about three times every year, were witness to the more stable relationships between the gangs, an opportunity for them to meet and trade on neutral territory. In addition, business would be transacted in the tents and deals done involving all aspects of their business. So the atmosphere at the site was more that of a twentieth century rock festival than anything else, with Bikers listening to music and swigging beer while workers looked after those whose indentures were to be sold.

The camp in which Lia and her companions were headed was almost in the centre of the clearing. Half a dozen tents had been erected, along with an area enclosed by a wall of canvas, in which they were to be kept. They were marched through a gap in the enclosure and halted inside. The grass was uncovered, and virtually the only furnishing consisted of a sort of sturdy fence that ran the length of the area. It was made of pine logs held together by steel bolts and concreted into the earth; a permanent fixture even when no auction was taking place.

Lia was placed at the far end of the fence, where she settled on the grass, glad of an opportunity of solitude. She lay back in the warm sun, her eyes closed, enjoying the peace. Before long she sensed a shadow falling on her and looked up to see Eva's serious face gazing down at her.

Eva was clearly unhappy with Lia's appearance, the dust and the wind of the journey having taken their toll. It was evident to Lia that Eva had been brought along to keep her looking her best for the sale, and she now set about her duties conscientiously. She fetched a large bowl of warm water and Lia was made to stand up in it while she was washed. She glowed red with embarrassment as Eva soaped her body in the presence of the others, rubbing the lather into her most private places then rinsing her down with more buckets of warm water. After that she knelt in the sunshine while Eva ran a comb through her long dark hair. Even her pubic hair was attended to, trimmed into a neat triangle and cut short to leave her sex lips more clearly visible.

No sooner had Eva finished Lia's ablutions than prospective buyers began to enter the enclosure. They came in their twos and threes at irregular intervals, some giving each one no more than a cursory glance, others lingering longer, asking questions, feeling muscles and inspecting teeth. Few of them showed much interest in Lia, though comments of the most intimate kind were made from time to time. Lia guessed it was workers they were interested in and whilst a young naked beauty might be an object of curiosity, she played no part in their business plans.

The visits went on for the rest of the day, the Bikers coming and going, with Eva fussing round her constantly, removing a fleck of grass here, replacing a stray hair there.

At last the sky began to redden and the visits became less and less. Outside the sound of revelry carried to them, with music, singing and drunken chants. A meal was brought, with Lia being served personally by Eva who sat and watched her eat, wiping her mouth afterwards and carrying off her plate. Then as it grew dark she took her leave, kissing Lia gently on the lips.

It was only after she left that Lia began to feel uneasy. The others had gathered at the far end of the compound and she realised they were whispering together and pointing in her direction. She turned away, pretending to ignore them. She wanted to sleep, but the bright security lights made it difficult. She surveyed the group covertly. They called over the man who'd been placed on guard and were talking to him in low voices, occasionally glancing at her. She strained to catch snatches of the conversation.

"...Bloody privileges, waited on hand and foot."

"...Got us into trouble in the first place..."

"...If you turn a blind eye... let you fuck her afterwards."

"...Five minutes, that's all we need..."

She turned away, frightened, and for once she would have welcomed the presence of one of the Bikers. She sat huddled against the post, wondering what would happen.

By the time she heard a movement behind her it was too late. As she turned someone grasped her arms, pinning back her elbows and a hand was placed firmly over her mouth. She struggled, lashing out with her legs and causing more than one of her attackers to curse in pain before more hands grabbed her ankles and she was subdued. Her head was pulled back, forcing her to look up, and she found herself gazing into Olga's face. The woman smiled at her without humour.

"So, where's your little lackey gone?"

Lia closed her eyes, refusing to meet Olga's.

"Proper little madam, aren't we, with a servant to fetch and carry? Look guys, she's got a hair out of place." She took hold of Lia's hair and yanked, causing tears of pain to spring to her eyes.

"And what's this, a bit of grass on her tit?" She grabbed Lia's nipple and pinched so that the girl squealed with pain through the hand that was gagging her. She took hold of Lia's hair again, dragging her face to within an inch of her own. "Why the hell should you get it so bloody easy? It's your fault we're here in the first place, Stefan and me. Now we've lost our rank and you're getting treated like a queen. Well I don't reckon you'll be worth much to anyone with half your teeth missing and your nose broken. Pull her up guys."

A chain was wrapped around Lia's throat and pulled so she could scarcely breathe. The men dragged her to her feet, holding her arms. Stefan stepped forward. He reached out and ran a hand over her cheek. "Very pretty," he said. "It won't look half as pretty with the jaw broken though. Hold her steady."

He began wrapping a length of chain round his fingers. He closed his fist, so that it formed a heavy gauntlet. Hands took hold of her head, holding it steady while he pulled back his fist. Lia closed her eyes.

Crunch! The force of the blow was tremendous, the crack of the breaking jawbone sickeningly loud. But it wasn't Lia's. She opened her eyes to see Stefan, his face covered in blood, staring stupidly at her before he slumped to the ground and lay still. A fist flashed past her head, felling one of the men that held her. The other let go at once, leaving her staggering, weak-kneed with shock. She tried to speak, but the earth seemed to be turning about her and she lost her balance, just aware of the strong hands that broke her fall as she slumped into unconsciousness.

She had no idea how long she was out, but guessed it was no more than a few minutes. She awoke to feel an arm about her, a hand stroking her hair.

She opened her eyes, but at first they were blurred and she was unable to make out the face close to hers. Then slowly it came into focus.

Thorkil! It was Thorkil!

She gasped, unable to believe her eyes. It was him! Her prince! He smiled down at her.

"Looks like I came along just in time. You seem to have a habit of getting into trouble."

"They... they were going to..."

"Shh. Don't even think about it." He glanced across at the rest of them cowering at the far end of the fence. "I doubt he'll ever be able to eat properly again, and that captive in charge will wish he was dead once Vargo hears of this."

"I... thank you," she said quietly.

"It was my pleasure. I'm just glad I chose to come when I did. Your face is far too pretty to be damaged like that."

She blushed, unable to think of how to reply. "Why are you here?" she asked at last.

"The same reason as everyone else. We need some mechanics and manual workers, so I'm here to buy their indentures."

"Oh." Her heart felt heavy. He was just like all the others.

"Mind you," he continued, "I did have it in mind to do a little personal shopping as well."

"You mean...?"

"Well, a man's entitled to a few luxuries, and I've got a bit of spare cash put by."

Her eyes widened. "You mean, you want me?"

"That was the general idea. Why, don't you approve?"

"Oh yes! Yes! Oh please do. Would it be for your very own?"

"My very own. You don't think I'd want to share you, do you?"

She wanted to fling her arms round him, but ended up blushing. He laughed, clutching her about the waist and pulling her to him.

"My own little pet," he whispered. "Should I keep you naked and chained?"

"If you wish," she replied. "I'll be all yours."

"Funny little thing," he said, and kissed her on the mouth, his tongue delving between her lips as she pressed herself closer to him.

They embraced for some time, she curled in his arms, enjoying his touch on her skin. His hands felt for her breasts, kneading them gently, teasing the nipples into life. She lay back from him slightly to give him better access. He smiled.

"You are a lovely young woman," he whispered.

She wriggled under his caresses. "And tomorrow I'll be yours."

"Yes. As long as Helda doesn't get you first."

"Helda?"

"The woman who runs the Black Cat."

She started, staring at him in alarm. "What do you mean?"

"Well, she's bound to be interested. Has she sent for you yet?"

"No."

"Well she will. Helda doesn't do the rounds like the rest of us. Her requirements are rather more specialist."

She wanted to ask him what the Black Cat was, but something made her hesitate. Then he was climbing to his feet.

"You're not going?"

"I have to. I've got more things to do. I'll see you tomorrow at the auction."

"But I thought we could..." She let the sentence trail away, embarrassed by her own lasciviousness.

He crouched down and ran his hand up her thigh, fingers gently probing her sex. "There'll be lots of time," he said. "Meanwhile you get some sleep. Don't forget that Helda is bound to send for you tomorrow."

"What will she do?"

"Inspect you," he said, and with that he was gone, leaving her with her thoughts. As she curled up on the grass something warm descended and she looked up to see Eva draping a blanket over her. She managed a smile, then dropped into a deep sleep.

She awoke with a start to find Eva fussing around her, a bowl of hot gruel in her hand. She was in a state of some agitation and Lia guessed at once that the summons from the mysterious Helda had arrived. She ate the gruel and allowed herself to be washed and groomed as before. This time Eva seemed to be taking particular care, and it was some time before she was satisfied.

At last Eva fitted Lia with cuffs and led her from the enclosure. Outside five or six others were already waiting to be chained together. Like Lia they had their hands fastened behind their backs with cuffs, and had chains hanging from their collars. A worker in grey overalls took the chain from Eva.

Lia expected to be led away but was shocked to feel her legs being forced apart and the chain pulled between them. It was arranged so that it dropped straight down between her breasts and under, the worker parting her sex lips and running it between her sex lips and up the valley of her arse, attaching it to the cuffs at her wrists. Lia tested the chain. She wished it had been attached more conventionally. There was something overtly sexual about the bondage. Every time she moved her hands the metal would rub against her clitoris. She tried to shut it from her mind, turning to watch as the others were similarly bound.

Surprisingly they were all male. She had expected to see mainly women, judging by what she had heard about Helda. She wondered about the discomfort the chain would cause them, squashing their genitals, but at least they had the protection of clothing.

Once all were bound they were attached together in a train, each linked to the other by a chain from their wrists to the collar of the one behind. In front of Lia was a stocky bearded man of about thirty who craned round to look at her, his eyes feasting hungrily on her bare breasts. He winked at her, then licked his lips and blew her a kiss. She felt him press closer to her, his hands feeling for her flesh. She tried to back away, but with the lead that attached her to him and the man behind there was nowhere to go. His wrists were pinned behind him at just the level of her sex, and she felt his fingers probing her unprotected sex, already moist with the action of the chain. She tried to hold her legs closed, to shut him out, but he persisted, worming his hands between her thighs. He slid his fingers over the chain, then worked them underneath it, folding the lips of her sex apart and feeling for her love bud.

As his actions became more bold they began to spark a reaction in her, a warmth beginning to fill her belly. He began teasing her clitoris. Lia felt her defences slipping under his caresses. Unable to control herself she leaned against him, widening her stance and rubbing her breasts on his back. He tilted his head back, his mouth close to her ear.

"I'd like to fuck you right now," he whispered. "I'd like to drape you over that fallen tree there and stuff my cock into that pretty little cunt you're so fond of flashing about."

Lia moaned quietly, stimulated by his coarse talk and the motion of his fingers on her sex.

"Then," he continued, "I'd suck those lovely tits of yours, and fill you with my spunk. Would you fancy that?"

"I... I..." Lia was at a loss for words. The thought of having sex there and then, of being brutally fucked on the tree in the open air thrilled her. She closed her eyes, thrusting against his fingers.

"What the hell are you playing at?" It was the man behind her, and she realised that every motion of her hips tugged on his collar. She straightened and tried to pull away, but the man had three fingers inside her now and she was unable to release herself.

"Please," she whimpered, but he paid no attention and again she felt her control slip.

Just at that moment the order was given to move off, and the man at the front stepped forward. The rest were pulled after him, many of them stumbling. Lia too was caught unawares and staggered a few paces before regaining her balance. Despite the motion the man in front of her retained his grip on her sex, his fingers deeply embedded, forcing Lia to walk with an awkward gait, her legs forced apart.

So they were marched across the camp, a rugged crew, heads down, chains rattling, the lovely girl in the centre making a strange contrast to her shabby neighbours. And as she walked she was being stimulated, trapped on the hand that manipulated her sex, trying her best to keep her hips from gyrating too much as the waves of passion spread through her.

They continued until they came to a group of tents on the far side of the clearing. There they were ordered to halt and await orders. The man went to work on Lia with renewed vigour, rubbing her swollen clitoris, making her juices flow more freely, his fingers making a squidgy noise as they worked back and forth.

"Keep still can't you? What's the matter?" It was the man behind again, once more disturbed as the thrusting of Lia's hips became more urgent. "Is he frigging you?"

Lia's answer was a moan as he raised her to new heights of lust.

"You filthy bitch." He turned to the man behind him. "Look at this. Bloody Lomax has got his fingers in her cunt and he's giving her a good frigging."

"Where?" Necks were craning round in front and behind, all trying to see what was happening. Lia tried half-heartedly to release herself again, but she knew she was too far gone, the manipulation too masterful for her to resist.

The line began bending round as those at the front and back tried to see what was happening. All eyes were on her and the prospect of being watched spurred her on still more. She was totally absorbed, her knees bent as she thrust herself on the hand, the lewd motions of her hips blatant as she felt her climax approaching. Her head was thrown back, eyes closed, her lips emitting short gasps, her breasts spasming as she shamelessly took her pleasure.

She could restrain herself no longer. The chains, her nakedness, the hand that held her so intimately and the eyes of the other captives upon her all combined to bring her to the peak, then push her over.

With a shout of passion she flung herself against the man, her orgasm filling her and overflowing in a wanton display of lust. "Yes, oh yes!" she cried as her juices flowed and the fervour of her climax overcame her. Oblivious to the sight she presented she continued to force her open sex against his fingers, her backside pumping back and forth as she milked every ounce of sensation from his rough hand. The sinews in her neck standing out, her mouth open and gasping for air, she spent herself against him, her motions slowing as she gradually came down from the heights, leaning against the man in front, gasping for breath, completely spent. She blushed as she realised the sight she must have made in front of the others.

"Yes, very nice. Well done Lomax. It seems all we've heard about this young lady is true."

A woman had emerged from the tent by which they had been standing. For a moment Lia could only stare. She was about thirty years old, tall and slim, her long hair dyed platinum blond under a black cap. She wore a leather jacket, covered in studs and superficially like those of the male Bikers, though it was beautifully cut and hugged her torso, her magnificent breasts swelling proudly from its low collar. Her skirt was leather too, and very short above the tops of her sheer black stockings. She wore high-heeled black boots, the toes tapering to a point. In her right hand was a cruel looking horse whip, which she slapped against her thigh. But it was her eyes that captivated

Lia. Bright green they seemed to flash from beneath long curling eyelashes as she smiled a cruel smile, her lips painted with purple lipstick.

Helda! This could only be Helda. Lia shrank back in fear as she realised in whose presence she was. She glanced round at her fellow captives, but far from showing fear they were laughing. She turned back to Helda, who was still smiling.

"I'm sorry, my dear. Just a little subterfuge to test your appetites. You'll be pleased to hear you came through with flying colours. I'm sure you'll be a most valuable addition to the Black Cat's staff." She turned to the man who had been escorting them. "All right, you can release them now."

Lia was flabbergasted. So the whole thing had been a set-up. No doubt Helda had been watching her all along. If only she had more control of her lusts!

The escort undid a catch on her collar, releasing Lomax. Helda ruffled his hair. "Good work. I'll see to it that you get your turn once she's ours." There was no doubting the implications of the statement.

The rest of the group was released and Lia stood alone, her head down. Helda walked around her, poking her with the whip, forcing her legs apart and lifting her breasts with it, her eyes all the time roving up and down Lia's body.

"Oh yes," she said. "Very nice. When were you last fucked?"

The question took Lia by surprise. She stared at the woman.

"Answer me!"

"Last week," Lia mumbled.

"Who by? What was his name?"

"I... I don't know his name. There were two of them."

"Two? And both of them fucked you? Where?"

"Only one. The other... I sucked the other."

"Where?"

"In the cab of their truck."

"This gets better and better. You took on two strangers in the cab of a truck. Then you let Lomax here frig you in front of everyone, then of course there's those videos in the storeroom. And don't look so surprised; there's not a lot goes on that doesn't come to my notice." She turned and shouted over her shoulder. "Fetch the table."

The flap of the tent was pulled aside and two men hurried out carrying a heavy wooden table between them. They placed it on the ground in front of Helda, then retreated.

"Lie on it."

Before she knew what was happening Lia was lifted and laid on her back, her arms trapped beneath her. Hands held her shoulders, pinning her down like some exotic biological specimen.

"Open your legs."

Lia obeyed, as wide as the chain between her ankles would allow. The shackle was undone and her legs were pulled wider apart towards the corners of the table. A second set of leg irons was produced and attached, the other ends fastened to the table legs so she was trapped, her sex open and available.

"That's better. Now, my dear, I want to see that active little cunt of yours properly. Offer it to me."

Lia's mind was a whirl. Offer it to her? What could she mean? She pushed her hips up uncertainly.

"Offer it to me, I said. As if you mean it."

Lia thrust up, pressing down with her ankles and lifting her backside clear of the table.

"That's better. Now hold it like that."

Lia remained as she was, watching Helda anxiously. The woman reversed the whip, revealing the gnarled bone handle, extending it towards Lia's sex. She held it for a moment against her lips, then pushed it inside, the rough surface sliding easily over the moist walls of her vagina. Lia gasped as she felt her juices flow round the object.

"Now grip it. Hard as you can."

Lia tensed the muscles of her sex, clamping the handle, its irregular surface stimulating her sensitive inner flesh as she enclosed it.

"That's it. Keep your legs open. Now grip tight. Go on."

Helda began pulling the whip, trying to remove it. Lia strained to keep it inserted, partly to please Helda and partly because of the delicious sensation its thick stem was arousing in her. Harder the woman pulled and harder she strained to hold it where it was, making a delightfully lewd display for the onlookers. Only her shoulders and heels resting on the table-top as she strained to win the erotic tug of war with the tall blonde.

Finally she could hold on no longer, and with a wet sound the whip handle came free, the juices from within the girl leaking out onto her open thighs.

"Very good. Very good indeed. I can see you'll be a real asset to my little organisation."

Lia said nothing, though in her heart she knew there would be another bidder for her that afternoon. She smiled inwardly as she thought how disappointed Helda would be when she saw her prize slip from her grasp.

It was to be another half hour before Lia was allowed to return to her enclosure. Helda had inspected every part of her body in the most intimate manner possible, probing and commenting on her assets to the captives who stood and watched. At last she appeared satisfied and released Lia from her confinement into the hands of Eva, who was clearly briefed to collect her.

As she stood in the enclosure while Eva gave her a final grooming before the auction, her heart was full of doubts. Supposing Thorkil failed to turn up? Or was unable to afford the price? She knew Helda was intent on procuring her and the testing inspection left her in little doubt as to the kind of duties she would be expected to carry out. Altogether it was a very anxious Lia who was led to the auction area by her silent little friend.

By the time they reached the arena the auction was in full swing. Dozens of Bikers and their privileged workers surrounded the rostrum on which the sale was taking place. One by one the forlorn lots were presented to the crowd and the bidding would begin, the climax of each sale being marked by the banging of a wooden gavel by the Biker conducting the transactions. Eva led Lia to the enclosure where she was to wait her turn.

Lia looked about anxiously. From where she was she could not see the whole crowd. She prayed Thorkil would be there waiting for her. She was struck by doubts. What had seemed a straightforward process the day before now seemed less certain amid the bustle and noise of the auction. She felt conspicuous, knowing she would be sold naked and thus attract extra attention.

One by one those ahead of her were leaving the enclosure and stepping up onto the rostrum, and Lia's turn was fast approaching. Only about a dozen remained, among them Olga, who appeared to be deep in conversation with a bearded man in grey overalls. It was Lomax. She watched as the two of them huddled together, occasionally glancing in her direction. The discussion went on for some time, then Lomax left and hurried away. Lia wondered what they could have been talking about. Certainly Lomax looked concerned when he left, and now Olga had a smug grin on her face as she stared defiantly across at Lia.

The sale continued and before long Olga was taken up to the dais. Soon Lia was the only one left, her heart beating hard as she awaited her turn. Then the sound of the gavel rang out and she was led forward.

Outside the sun shone brightly and Lia blinked as she was led up the steps. Despite the fact that the sale was nearly at an end the crowd had remained, anxious for a glimpse of her and curious to see how the bidding would go. She reached the platform and Eva led her to the box on which she was to stand while the bidding ensued. She climbed up and stood surveying the crowd, searching for her prince.

The auctioneer began his sales patter. "Here, ladies and gentlemen, you have our last item for sale today, and as you can see this one comes with no hidden extras." The crowd laughed but the remark scarcely registered with Lia, who was still searching for Thorkil.

The auctioneer came to the end of his introduction and the bidding began. At first the bids were small, a few hopefuls trying their luck, but as the stakes grew higher so they dropped out until only a few remained, and still Lia had heard nothing from Thorkil.

"Fifteen thousand." The bid came from a Biker who stood on the edge of the crowd, squinting at the girl on the rostrum. For a moment her heart leapt, but he was nothing like Thorkil.

The crowd went quiet, the auctioneer scanning the faces for a counter bid. Lia's heart stood still. She hadn't expected this at all. Where was Thorkil?

"Sixteen." A chill went down Lia's spine as she recognised Helda's voice.

"Seventeen thousand."

The bidding continued. Eighteen, nineteen, twenty, twenty-five. Still it went up. Only the Biker and Helda were in the race now, the rest of the crowd silent as they watched the duel. Lia just stood where she was, unable to believe what was happening - that she had been deserted.

The price rose; thirty thousand, forty thousand. Helda was becoming visibly agitated as the man continued to outbid her. The price reached fifty-three thousand, and Helda hesitated for the first time.

The auctioneer waited for a moment. "Fifty-three," he intoned. "Fifty-three thousand. Any advance?" Still there was no response from Helda.

Lia held her breath, waiting for the hammer to drop. "Fifty-three. Going once at fifty-three thousand. Going twice."

"Fifty-four," said Helda, in a voice just loud enough for the auctioneer to hear.

Lia turned expectantly towards the Biker. Even he would be better than Helda. But she recognised the look of defeat in his eyes as he turned away.

"Going once for fifty-four thousand." The auctioneer paused. "Going twice... gone!" He brought down the gavel with a bang that resounded around Lia's head. Her shoulders slumped. She belonged to Helda!

Chapter 10

The Black Cat

When Lia awoke she found herself in a sprung bed, the sheets clean, the eiderdown smelling fresh and expensive. She snuggled against the pillows, luxuriating in their softness after the hard bunk she had been used to. She closed her eyes again and dozed, slipping in and out of sleep, her tired mind unwilling to confront her situation, content only to enjoy the unexpected calm in what had become a far from settled period in her life.

The room brightened as the day progressed, but the sleepy girl dozed on, the accumulated weariness of the past few weeks, coupled with the drug she had been administered, keeping her docile.

It was nearly midday before she finally rose from the bed, wandering dazedly across the room to gaze from the window. The room looked onto a garden, the trees and shrubs well kept. In the distance she could see two or three gardeners going about their work. She turned away, exploring the room further.

The carpet was thick and expensive, springy beneath her bare feet. The furnishings were elegant and plush, the walls hung with sporting prints. In one corner was a television and video, with a rack of tapes. Lia slipped one into the machine and turned it on. The scene was of a naked girl tied to a tree being fucked by a rough looking man, while beside them a second naked beauty was being whipped. Lia sat back on her heels and watched for a while.

She turned the machine off and continued to explore the room. On the far side was a door, beyond which she could see a bathroom. She went inside. It was large, with a sunken tub against one wall. She turned a tap and hot water gushed out. It was a long time since she'd had the opportunity to soak in a proper tub and the water looked inviting. She left the tap running while she explored the cabinet over the basin. Inside she found a bottle of bubble bath, which she poured in. Then she climbed into the warm, luxurious water, lying back and closing her eyes, enjoying the feel of rich suds washing round her.

As she soaked she tried to remember how she got where she was, searching her memory for some clue. She remembered the auction and that dreadful sound as the gavel banged, confirming her sale to Helda. Then she had been led from the platform, allowed only a glance at sobbing Eva as she was whisked away to Helda's tent.

She soaked for about twenty minutes, then climbed out and dried herself on a large towel that was attached to the towel rail by a strong silken cord. She stood in front of the full length mirror examining herself. If anything the hardships of the last weeks had improved her figure. Her skin was somehow softer and she had lost a little weight, her slim hips accentuating the swell of her breasts. Her bum was firmer too.

She wandered back into the bedroom. There was a door in the wall opposite the bed and she tried the handle. It turned and the door swung open. She peered out into a long hallway. On the floor was another thick carpet and on each side were more doors, each bearing a brass number plate. There was no one in sight.

She stepped out into the corridor. Behind her the door shut with a click. Instantly she tried the handle, but she was locked out. She cursed herself for not finding something to wear first.

She set out to the left, moving noiselessly along the carpet in her bare feet. At the end was a double door which opened into another hallway. She kept going, trying the doors occasionally but finding them all locked. She came to a staircase and descended. At the bottom was another door which led into a passage altogether different from the one she had just left. The doors here were made of bars, like those in the depot, and the floor was bare. She turned down another corridor, through another pair of doors, then stopped.

She could hear a noise. The sound of raised voices and a banging and crashing, as if some kind of heavy work was in progress. She crept closer and the smell of cooking assailed her nostrils, reminding her of how hungry she was. Ahead was a pair of green doors with a small window in each. She crept closer, and standing on tiptoe gazed through.

It was a kitchen. All around were pots and pans of various shapes and sizes. In the middle were great stoves on which a myriad of dishes were bubbling away, the source of the delicious smells. The kitchen was a hive of activity, with workers stirring, chopping, kneading or washing up in great white sinks. But Lia's eyes were on the food. She licked her lips. How she would love a bowl of stew with a hunk of freshly baked bread. She wondered if she could go in, possibly on the pretence of being a kitchen worker, and grab something to eat. But how could she? She was naked. She stood with her nose pressed to the glass, watching.

Looking down she noticed a table just inside the door. On it was a loaf of bread. If only she could open the door a tad she might just be able to reach inside and grab it. Then she could be off back down the corridor with no one the wiser. She looked about. They were all intent on their work. She took a deep breath. It was now or never.

She eased open the door about six inches, peering through the crack. There was the loaf, about three feet away. She stretched out her arm towards it, hoping desperately that no one would be looking her way. Just a few more inches and nobody had turned round. She reached a little further and her hand closed on the bread. She snatched it back and turned to run, bumping straight into someone.

"Well, well, a sneaky thief, eh?" He was about twenty, with long hair and wearing overalls spotted with grease.

She coloured deeply. "No, I... I was just..."

"Just stealing from the kitchen by the look of it."

"I... I was..." She dried up in the face of his arrogant confidence, her eyes dropping to the loaf in her hands.

"What? You're not telling me you weren't stealing it. Anyhow, by the look of you it's clothes you should be after. Do you always walk about like that?"

"I..."

Suddenly he moved close, grabbing her wrists, the force of his grip hurting her. He held her arms apart, his eyes roving over her body. He grinned at her discomfort. "I think we'd better see the cook about this," he said. He dragged her into the heat and bustle of the busy kitchen, shouting as he went. "Look what I've found, guys!"

The kitchen workers turned to see what the fuss was about as he thrust the naked girl in front of him. She stood, helpless as they crowded around her.

"What's she doing here?"

"What a lovely pair of tits."

"Do you think she's looking for some fun?"

"I'll certainly give her some."

Lia backed against a wall as they came closer, their comments becoming more coarse. Some of them were reaching out for her, prodding and poking. She closed her eyes, fearful of what they would do as the noise grew. Then a stronger voice cut through the clamour.

"What the hell's going on here?"

Lia looked up to see a tall man thrusting his way through the crowd. The workers fell away as he came through. He was in the grey overall of a privileged worker, and Lia guessed he was the cook.

He reached where Lia was cowering and turned to the others. "Get back to work!" he shouted.

With a murmur of discontent they turned away, returning to their tasks, all but the one who had found her, who held his ground.

The newcomer confronted Lia. "What are you doing here?"

"I'm sorry..." she said lamely.

The young man broke in. "She was stealing. She took a loaf of bread. Look, it's still in her hands."

"Is this true?" The cook's eyes darkened.

"I was lost. And hungry. I'm sorry. I don't know where I am. Here, you can have it back." She offered him the loaf.

"So you did take it." He snatched it from her. "This is a serious offence, stealing from the kitchens. Where do you work?"

"I don't know. I only arrived yesterday."

"That's no excuse. I'll have to report this." He turned to the young man. "Art, I want you to take her to the office. Get me some cuffs."

The young man was gone for a few moments, then reappeared with a pair of handcuffs which he proceeded to snap onto her wrists behind her back.

The cook tested the locks. "Right," he said, "up to the office while I make my report."

Art leered at her. "Can I take her the scenic route?"

"Just take her there and come straight back. And keep your hands off."

Art shrugged and said to her, "That way," indicating the door.

Lia retraced her steps through the corridors and up the stairs, then through another door. All the time he was close behind, guiding her, his hands wandering across the pliant skin of her backside in the pretence of hurrying her along. At last they reached a room marked *Administration*, where Art ordered her to stop.

He turned her round, pinning her against the wall. "That's the place," he said, his eyes roving hungrily over her body. "By now they'll be expecting you." He stroked her breasts, leaning down so his mouth was beside her ear. "I'll fuck you before the week's out," he vowed, in a low voice. "Just you wait and see."

With that he was gone, leaving Lia standing nervously outside the door, her mind in a whirl. She gazed about, seeking a way of escape, but there was nothing else for it. Drawing a deep breath she turned round and tapped on the door with her bound hands, then pulled down the handle, pushed with her backside and entered.

The room had no carpet and was almost bare, reminding her of the offices at the depot. The sole item of furniture was a low counter behind which stood a man. He eyed her up and down for a moment.

"Ah," he said at last. "Been sent from the kitchen, I believe. We've been expecting you." He opened a door behind the counter and gestured to her. "Through here."

Lia followed him. The contrast with the outer office was striking. The floor was thickly carpeted, the walls hung with pictures. For a moment she was struck by the similarity with Vargo's office at the depot, but to one side was a large mahogany desk and behind it sat a commanding figure. It was Helda.

The man shoved Lia forward, and she walked uncertainly up to the desk.

"There you are, my dear." Helda bared her teeth in a grim smile. "Welcome to the Black Cat. I trust you were comfortable last night?"

Lia nodded.

"Yes, I thought I'd let you enjoy one of our guestrooms for the night," Helda continued. "After all, you'll be frequenting them often enough, though not alone of course. Now what's this about a loaf of bread?"

Lia opened her mouth to explain, but her throat was dry and no words would come.

"I'm told you were caught stealing a loaf from the kitchen. Is this true?"

Lia nodded again, her heart pounding.

"What a shame to start on such a bad footing. You'll have to be punished, of course." A faint smile played on Helda's lips. "This evening, I think. It'll be a good introduction. Besides, it's most popular with the clients." She looked up at the man, who was still standing by the door. "I think we'll have one of our little raffles, Philippe. See to it." The man nodded.

"Now..." Helda turned her penetrating eyes on Lia once more. "You can start work this evening in the club, clearing the tables." She scanned Lia up and down. "I suppose we'll have to find something for you to wear. Meanwhile I think we'll have that pussy of yours shaved; it makes your intentions so much clearer. Besides, we haven't had a shaven girl here for a while. All right, Philippe, take her away."

Lia felt her arm gripped from behind. The interview was at an end, though she was little the wiser about her fate. A raffle - what could that possibly mean? And what would it have to do with her punishment? She barely registered where she was as she was whisked down the hallway by Philippe.

They came to a halt outside a room marked *Preparation*. Philippe opened the door and pushed her inside. A man in a bath towel greeted them.

"Yes?" His voice was soft and slightly effeminate.

"This one's new. She's working in the club tonight. Have her shaved and cleaned up, then find her something to wear. She's due for punishment so make it suitable."

The man smiled and gave Lia a mock bow. "My pleasure." Philippe went out, leaving the two of them alone. The man unlocked her cuffs and thrust a bar of soap into her hand. "Go in there and shower, then come back here and I'll do your hair properly."

The shower was warm, the powerful jets playing on her skin, making it tingle. She lingered in the cubicle, towelling herself down for the second time in a matter of hours. Then wrapping the towel around herself she returned to where the man was waiting.

"Come along," he fussed, leading her into another room, brightly lit and furnished with chairs like those in a hairdressing salon. Two were already occupied by other girls, similarly clad in towels, their heads partly obscured by hairdryers. They scarcely registered Lia's arrival. The man indicated one of the empty chairs and Lia sat in it.

He swung the chair round so her head was over a basin and proceeded to shampoo her hair. After that it was rinsed and treated with sweet smelling conditioners, before the drier was pulled down over her head. A girl knelt beside the chair and manicured her nails, while the man gathered a shaving brush and razor.

"Right," he said, "let's have that towel." Lia blushed as she reluctantly bared her body yet again, but he was matter-of-fact. "Now move forward so your bum's right on the edge of the seat. That's right. Legs apart, don't be shy."

Lia was aware of the other two girls scrutinising her as she adopted the revealing position. The man began brushing lather into her pubic hair, his fingers working expertly around her sex lips. Then he picked up the razor, sweeping it up and down a leather strop a few times, before leaning over her.

The razor was cold and she winced slightly as she felt it on her skin, scraping across her pubic mound. She watched as he inched his way around, a pile of lather and hairs building up in front of the blade. He worked quickly and skilfully, sliding the instrument over her then sloshing it about in a mug of water. She held perfectly still as he worked, trying hard not to respond to his inadvertently stimulating caresses.

At last he was finished. He wiped her with a damp cloth and stood back to admire his handiwork. It felt strange and she stroked a hand over herself, amazed at the increased sensitivity. Meanwhile he removed the dryer from her hair and began combing it out. She wanted to ask for the towel back, but instead just sat and allowed him to groom her.

Finally he seemed satisfied, and led her to a full length mirror. Lia stood transfixed. She had never felt so naked before. Gone was the dark triangle and in its place just bare skin so that the lips of her vagina were clearly visible. Now she understood what Helda had meant about making her intentions clear. Having her sex so bare seemed to constitute a blatant invitation to anyone seeing her.

He smiled, standing beside her and admiring her in the mirror too. "Very nice," he said. "Now let's see about that costume."

He led her into another room, this one lined with cupboards and racks of clothes. He scrutinised the shelves. "Let's see, for the club," he mused, "and due to be punished. I think something a little neanderthal might fit the bill."

He pulled something from one of the cupboards and handed it to her. At first it looked to her like a brown rag, but as it unfolded it began to take shape. Made of very soft leather, like chamois, the top hung from one shoulder and draped over her breasts. It was so short that the undersides of her bottom were clearly visible beneath the hem. She gazed at herself in the mirror. The leather and the ragged hem reminded her of a film she had seen once, with a cavewoman dressed like she was who fought battles with somewhat anachronistic dinosaurs.

Having satisfied himself that she was fully presentable, the man picked up a telephone and tapped out a number. He spoke for a few moments then replaced the receiver.

"I'm to take you for something to eat before you start. Come on."

The canteen was almost deserted and Lia guessed they were late, from the surly compliance of the server. But the food was good and Lia gulped it down hungrily. When at last she'd had enough she sat back and turned to the man. "What's your name?"

"Cyrian."

"Tell me about the Black Cat, Cyrian."

"You mean you don't know?"

She shook her head.

"Well you'll soon find out." He seemed reluctant to tell her more, as if afraid he would scare her.

"What happens?"

"It's a sort of nightclub, really. The people from the city come. Helda arranges buses here, and back at the end of the evening, and in the morning."

"City people?"

"Yes. Well they can't get the kind of... entertainment, Helda can give. There are laws in the city, you see."

"Against what?"

He clearly felt he had said enough. "Come on," he said. "It's getting late."

The noise of the club was audible from some distance away as they hurried down the corridor, the loud music resounding through the halls. At last they reached a room with the sign *Scullery* on the door. Cyrian opened it, and inside the noise was even louder, so they were forced to shout.

"Here we are," bawled Cyrian. "Lotti here will tell you what to do." He Indicated a bored girl who sat by the door, smoking. She wore a black maid's uniform, the skirt cut well above the knees. She looked Lia up and down.

"What the hell you dressed for, hunting mammoths?" She laughed at her own joke for a moment, then became more business-like. "Right, our job's to keep the tables clear of empty plates and glasses, encourage them to eat or drink more. Just get out there and bring them in, then put them through there." She indicated a hatch in the wall and, peering through, Lia saw it led into the kitchen she had been in earlier. "And mind their hands," she shouted over her shoulder as she shoved open the doors that led into the club. Lia followed her in.

Inside the noise was incredible. The room was filled with tables, every one packed with people, mainly young men eating and drinking and making shouted conversation. The decor was predominantly black, with erotic friezes on the walls. They were lit by fluorescent lights, making them glow eerily.

The subjects were numerous; men with women, women with women, the combinations seemingly endless. The rest of the lighting was subtle, with bright pools on the floor made by spotlights set in the ceiling. At one end was a small stage where a bikini-clad girl was dancing slowly in the glare of footlights.

As well as the men a number of women were standing about or sitting at the bar. Some were at the tables or on the men's laps, laughing with them. Lia guessed they too worked here.

She set about her work, clearing the bottles, glasses and plates. The work seemed endless. No sooner was one table cleared than another was full. Lia struggled in and out of the pantry, her arms laden with crockery, deftly avoiding the groping hands that reached for her as she passed.

The evening continued. Every now and then Lia noticed one or two of the girls disappearing with customers through a door at the end of the room. She thought of the comfortable rooms upstairs, realising their purpose. Most of the customers stayed put; drinking, talking and eating and watching the dancers on stage. Lia felt the tension in the room was beginning to rise, and noticed many of them examining their watches. Then, as she carried yet another tray of glasses into the scullery she felt a hand on her arm. It was Philippe.

"Time to come with me, my little lovely," he said. "They're waiting for the raffle to be drawn."

Lia felt a chill in the pit of her stomach as she followed him back into the club. She noticed the music had stopped and the chatter was down to a low hubbub. Philippe led her up a small flight of steps into the wings of the stage. Then as the spotlight came on he walked out.

"Ladies and gentlemen, as you are no doubt aware we are holding one of our little raffles tonight. The young lady in question was caught stealing from the kitchen today, so naturally she's due for punishment."

A cheer went up from the audience. Lia watched in confusion. What was going to happen to her?

Philippe was still talking. "I hope you all have your admission tickets ready, ladies and gentlemen, because here is the young lady herself to make the draw." He beckoned to Lia to join him on the stage. Her mind spinning she stepped out into the spotlight.

The cheers became even louder. Lia felt terribly vulnerable in the harsh light before all the people. She wished she had something more substantial to wear, aware that the costume was more provocative than modest. She realised Philippe was holding something in front of her and looked down to see a bag full of folded pieces of paper. She stared at it, unsure.

Then it dawned on her. The raffle! The winner was to inflict her punishment! No wonder the crowd was in such a tense state. She looked out over the sea of expectant eyes, at the faces, any one of whom could soon be whipping her. She remained watching them as a silence descended, unwilling to break the tension, somehow stimulated by being the centre of attention. She realised with a shock that the whole situation was turning her on!

She looked down again at the bag, then out at the expectant faces, and strangely anxious to know who would be the lucky winner, she plunged her arm into the bag. She rummaged about for a moment, then withdrew a ticket. She carefully unfolded it and read the number, looking up at the silent audience. "Two hundred and forty-three!" she shouted.

The silence continued for a moment longer, then a single cheer went up, followed by a number of other cheers from the same table. An arm was waving a small piece of paper. Lia's chastiser was making himself known. He began making his way forward, egged on by his friends, clambering up the steps to stand beside them on the platform.

He stood about six foot tall. His hair was short and he wore an earring in his left ear. His face was rugged, weathered by the sun, and Lia guessed he worked outdoors; probably a construction worker, as his muscular arms and rough hands seemed to confirm. He wore a T-shirt with short sleeves and a pair of jeans buckled well down his hips by a broad leather belt. He seemed to tower over the girl as she stood awaiting the next move.

Philippe began interviewing him. His name was Dave, he lived in the city and he was indeed a builder. He was here with a party of friends from work. All the time they talked Lia stood gazing at him, at the strong arms and the broad chest. She could smell his maleness over the cheap aftershave he wore, and an animalistic feeling rose within her as she considered her fate.

The charade went on a little longer, with more mundane questions being asked. Then Lia was asked to feel his muscles, which were firm and hard, and she found the physical attraction increase. Then the formalities were over, there was a roll of drums and the spotlight switched to a set of curtains above and to the back of the stage. Two other girls appeared by her side, taking an arm each. Lia resisted for a second, then allowed herself to be led backstage. There she was taken up a flight of steps that led to a second stage.

She stepped into the darkness behind the curtains, blinded after the spotlights below. Then with a snap the stage lights came on, and her heart skipped a beat as she observed the tableau revealed.

The stage was decorated like a dungeon, the walls black and streaked with damp. All around chains hung from rings on the wall and high above was a small barred window. She shuddered at the sight of it. The room was dominated by a great wooden frame in the centre, from which hung chains and shackles. The frame stood on a platform about three feet above the level of the stage, with a small flight of steps up the side, and it was to this that she was being taken.

Lia stood passive on the platform as they prepared her for the punishment. One of the girls took her hands and fastened shackles around her wrists. Then they were hauled up to the upper corners of the frame. The second girl secured her ankles in a similar manner, pulling her legs apart so when they were finished she was stretched helpless in a figure X on the frame. Having checked that the clamps on her wrists and ankles were tight and secure the two attendants retired to opposite sides of the stage, where they stood like sentries over their charge.

Behind the curtains Lia could hear the music building to a climax. Her heart raced as she thought of the spectacle that was about to be presented to the crowd below, yet all the time there was that warm feeling in her belly and that sense of expectancy of something exciting about to happen.

The curtains swept apart and the cheers of the crowd were all around her. She blinked into the bright spotlight, barely able to discern the sea of faces turned towards her. She heard footsteps to her right and saw Philippe address Dave in a loud stage voice.

"Here is the miscreant. She is to be given eight strokes with the horsewhip. Then she is yours to do with as you please."

These last words gave Lia a strange feeling in the pit of her stomach and made a familiar wetness well up between her thighs.

Phillippe withdrew, leaving the man standing beside the frame. He turned to the attendants. "Strip her," he said loudly.

The girls hesitated, looking for guidance to Philippe, who stood in the wings, so Lia guessed this was not necessarily a part of the plan. However he nodded almost imperceptibly and the two climbed the steps. The crowd fell silent.

The girls undid the knot at Lia's shoulder and the top slid from her, revealing her lovely breasts to the spellbound audience. Already the thrill of exposure was having its effect on her and as they watched her nipples swelled, standing erect and inviting.

The skirt fell away, leaving her shaven sex exposed, the wetness glistening under the bright lights. The crowd gasped, pointing and commenting to one another.

The two girls descended from the platform and returned to the sides of the stage. Responding to the calls from below they threw Lia's meagre garment down to the onlookers, who fought for it, anxious for souvenirs.

Dave mounted the platform. He stood before the helpless girl, taking her chin in his hand and raising her face to his. His hand slipped down her neck to her breasts, which he enclosed in a rough grip, kneading them, watching Lia's face as she responded to his touch. His hand fell lower, sliding over the bare skin of her pubic mound, his fingers penetrating her vagina so that she sighed with the sensation, pushing her hips against his probing.

For a moment he held her, working on the delicious sensations he aroused in her. Then he released her and bending the whip in his hands, stood back. He ran its leather tip over her erect nipples for a moment, then drew back his arm.

Whack! The whip came down on her backside, her body rocked forward. She was surprised at how little pain she felt, and looked at Dave quizzically, who grinned at her. Clearly he had received orders from Philippe that the Black Cat's new prize merchandise was not to be too badly damaged.

Whack! A second blow fell across her bare behind, the sound of the strike echoing around the silent walls. Again Lia made no sound, holding her head up and staring out into the spotlight.

Whack! The third stroke fell across her back just above the swell of her bottom, making her draw breath sharply as it fell. Then she felt Dave's hand push between her open legs from behind, his fingers penetrating her open sex in full view of the audience. She made a low moaning sound as she pressed against him, working her hips back and forth on his hand. He withdrew and she braced herself again.

Whack! The fourth blow caught her at the top of her legs, making the chains rattle as her body convulsed. She bit her lip, knowing there were still four more to come.

Whack! This time it was the full globes of her bottom that took the force of the blow. She was sweating now, her trussed body shining in the bright lights.

Whack! She cried out, anxious to please the spellbound crowd, to make them feel the pain was worse than it was, her squeal ringing around the club. She felt the hand probing her once again and the feelings of pain and lust seemed to merge into one as she thrust her hips onto his hand. He prised her outer lips apart and she felt her clitoris swelling, knowing the crowd could see clearly the extent of her stimulation. This time when he removed his hand she could not control the convulsions as her sex tried to close around an imaginary cock.

Whack! Lia screamed as the whip fell. This time the sting was real, and she tried to blot it from her mind, concentrating instead on the erotic sight her naked and spread-eagled body must be making for the men below.

Whack! The final blow fell with some force. She writhed in the chains, her body bathed in sweat that trickled from her in droplets. She was breathing heavily, exhausted, but still she found the strength to raise her head, and gazed defiantly out over the crowd.

There was silence for a moment longer, then a cheer rang around the room as Dave took a bow, turning to Lia and kissing her lips, his tongue probing into her mouth as his hands mauled her bare breasts. She responded enthusiastically to the kiss, thoroughly turned on by the whole situation, willing him to caress her sex again.

He stood back and beckoned to the attendants, who came forward, releasing her hands, then her ankles, and she stood rubbing her sore wrists, enjoying the attention of the crowd.

"Give her one, Dave!"

"Yeah, fuck the bitch. She sure looks like she's on heat."

Lia's stomach began to churn again at the crude shouts. The thought of being screwed so publicly, up on this stage before all these people seemed incredible, yet she knew she would be unable to control herself if he did. She could already feel her juices flowing at the thought of it.

He looked at her, flexing the whip. "You wanna be fucked?"

She hesitated, then nodded, blushing furiously at her own wantonness.

"Say it aloud."

"Please fuck me," she said quietly.

"Louder."

"Please fuck me."

"Louder. Plead with me."

"For pity's sake, Dave!" she shouted. "Please for pity's sake fuck me! Please!"

He grinned, and to a cheer from the audience began unbuckling his belt. As he dropped his jeans Lia was able to control her feelings no longer. Kneeling at his feet she reached into his briefs. His penis was thick and long, and already rising to attention as she pulled it out. She gazed at it for a moment, marvelling at the great vein that throbbed within and the swollen purple head. Then she had taken it in her mouth and was sucking it greedily, her hands working the foreskin up and down while the crowd continued to shout encouragement.

He allowed her to suck him for a while, then grabbed her hair, pulling back her head. "Back over the there," he ordered, indicating with a nod where he wanted her.

Obediently she stretched herself forward across the platform, her backside presented to her audience. She felt him grip her hips, then without ceremony his penis thrust inside her, penetrating her, making her shout out with passion as he drove further in, stretching the walls of her vagina with his stiff rod.

Then he was pumping his cock in and out, his organ sliding easily over her wetness as she pushed back against him. She gazed over her shoulder at the rapt expression on his face as he shafted her, his hands grasping her hips, his arse heaving back and forth as he took his pleasure in her. Her eye caught one of the attendants, who stood watching the performance with fascination. Lia stared into the girl's eyes as if challenging her to criticise her wanton behaviour. She licked her lips and winked, causing the girl to drop her eyes in embarrassment.

Dave's thrusts were coming faster and harder and Lia sensed his climax approaching. Still she held her body under control, contracting the muscles of her vagina around his cock, knowing it increased his pleasure. She heard his breathing increase and felt his body stiffen, then he was coming, spurts of warm semen washing into her vagina as he shoved his cock deep, the slapping of his abdomen against the cheeks of her arse making her rock with the force of his orgasm. She cried out with the pleasure of it all, but still held back her own climax, desiring to prolong it as long as she was able.

His thrusts were slowing as the last of his sperm pumped into her, and she sensed him relaxing. She remained as she was, letting him extract his enjoyment from her, as was his right, having won her. At last he withdrew, sliding his cock from her. She turned, and kneeling once more took him in her mouth, tasting the cocktail of her own juices and his sperm as she licked him. Then she leaned back on her knees, legs parted with her hands behind her head, awaiting her next order.

The crowd cheered as Dave refastened his trousers, a look of satisfaction on his face. He gazed down at the girl kneeling at his feet, her thighs streaked with wetness, her breasts swollen, the nipples proudly erect, her arse red from its recent beating. He pulled her to her feet and shoved her to the edge of the platform. "Who's next?" he called.

A great shout went up as hands reached to grasp her ankles. Lia staggered for a moment, nearly losing her balance, then she felt Dave's hands under her armpits as he lifted her effortlessly and lowered her to the floor below, down among the excited audience.

The men jostled in closer, groping at her body. She tried to back away but there were more behind her, stroking her and reaching for her breasts. She felt her arms pinned to her sides as she struggled. Hands were reaching from all angles as the men redoubled their efforts to get at her. Her legs were grabbed and fingers delved inside her.

She was borne aloft, carried across the room and deposited on her back across a table. Hands pulled her legs apart, others forcing the lips of her sex open. Then she felt a rigid penis forcing its way between her thighs and one of the men was inside her, fucking her hard, his hips thrusting against her as he satisfied himself.

Scarcely had she registered it than another man climbed astride her body on the table, forcing his cock into her mouth. She took it in, closing her lips about it, struggling against the hands that pinned her arms, anxious to feel his balls in her hands. She began working his organ in and out of her mouth, trying to match the rhythm of the man inside her sex. Her mind was a whirl as she lay naked and vulnerable on the table of the dingy club while the men queued to have their way with her. This was what her job entailed now, she thought, and she was determined to be the best.

Suddenly she felt a second helping of sperm squirting into her vagina. She gave a cry of pleasure, partly stifled by the throbbing cock in her mouth.

Almost at once another penis was invading her sex, but she had no time to think about it as her mouth was being filled with semen too. She sucked hungrily, emptying him of his seed, then he was gone and another was clambering over her, assaulting her mouth with his organ.

Lia had no idea how long she lay pinned to the table while her body was penetrated from both ends. She lost count of the number of men who pumped their seed into her, of her own orgasms which, now she had relaxed, came one after another as she took her lascivious pleasure there on the table.

At one stage she was carried out into the garden and plunged into a jacuzzi where she managed to wash some of the sperm from her. Then she was dragged out and fucked on the grass, before being carried inside once more. One man had her on the dance floor, her legs wrapped around his waist as he carried her on his stiff rod, bouncing her up and down to the rhythm of the music. Another took her from behind while she licked the vagina of his girlfriend. Another made her squeeze her breasts together while he pushed his penis between them, depositing his spunk onto her face and hair. Lia simply abandoned herself to pleasure, letting them pass her from one to the other to do with her as they wished, revelling in her exposure and wantonness amongst the roomful of strangers.

As the night went on she began to feel weary. She lay back on a divan in one corner, almost dozing, impassive as those who had gained a second wind took their pleasure in her again. The whole scene was almost dreamlike; the pulsing of the music, the lights, the lovers, and she drifted into an exhausted sleep.

She came back to consciousness gently with the familiar feel of a cock penetrating her. She moaned slightly, her eyes still shut as her body responded to the sensations and her muscles closed around the organ in response, allowing an orgasm to pulse through her as she felt him come. She was struck then by the silence, the absence of the music. She opened her eyes, blinking with the brightness of daylight and tried to focus on the face of her lover. It was Art, from the kitchen. He grinned at her as he withdrew.

"Hi," he said. "I was just passing and couldn't resist it. Besides, I told you I would."

With that he was gone, leaving her staring after him.

Chapter 11

The Escape

During the next few weeks Lia's life began to settle into a sort of pattern at the Black Cat. After her ordeal in the club she was shown to her cell and allowed to sleep for twenty-four hours.

The following morning she was bathed and shaved and put into the hands of a photographer who spent most of the morning taking shots of her. He posed her on the bed, on chairs, on the floor, in the gardens. He had her chained over a sort of vaulting horse, and had her given two hard strokes with a thin cane. Then he shot her looking back at the camera, the cane placed prominently beside her. He took more photos of her in chains, and even photographed her staked out on the lawn, her body spread wide and inviting.

The photos were to be used in a sort of catalogue that was kept in the foyer of the Black Cat for visitors to peruse when finding the companion of their choice. Each entry consisted of a portfolio of photos, along with a short write-up on the particular slave. Every slave had some sort of speciality. One wore a nurse's uniform, another the leather outfit and boots of a dominatrix, and so on.

Lia was taken to the foyer and allowed to read her own entry the following week. She found a set of gratuitously lewd shots of herself, her shaven sex prominent, her expressions salacious. On one, taken from behind, the glistening wetness of her sex lips betrayed her lascivious nature. The write up too, was alluring.

This is Lia, one of our latest acquisitions and one we are sure you will find delightful. Lia has an insatiable appetite for sex and was originally discovered wandering completely naked along the highway exposing herself to truck drivers, then allowing them to have their way with her lovely body in their cabs. Unlike our other offerings, Lia possesses no clothes, preferring to be naked at all times. All the better to meet the needs of anyone wishing to fuck her! She even keeps her cunt shaven, so as to allow a better view of what she is offering and will submit willingly to your desires, indoors or outside, in private or public. As can be seen, she requires disciplining frequently for her sexual excesses, and submits regularly to the whip. Should you be in any way dissatisfied with her services, facilities can be made available for you to punish her as you wish.

Lia read the words a number of times. In a sense it was all true; she certainly possessed no clothes and her shaven sex was an invitation to anyone who saw it. As for the punishments, they had become a part of her life now and she had come to rely on them.

She soon slipped into the routine of the Black Cat. Mornings were generally spent sleeping after the late nights with the club guests. In the afternoon she would be taken to Cyrian to be bathed and shaved, then she would await her evening's work. Some nights she would be taken to one of the luxurious rooms to entertain a guest who had requested her specifically. Others she would be called to the club, though after the excesses of her first night this was generally to visit a party in a private room. Some evenings she would be the escort of a single man, either in the club or the adjoining casino. At all times she was completely naked and was expected to obey the orders of her companions.

This might consist of simply sleeping with them. Others were content to flaunt the naked beauty on their arm to all envious watchers, occasionally fucking her publicly in the club or the gardens or offering her to another, content to stand and watch. Some would beat her, or ask her to perform strange acts like sucking their toes or sitting on their faces. When she was sent to a private party it inevitably resulted in her submitting to a number of men, being passed around the table, sitting astride each one in turn.

Young Art continued to feature in her life as well. One morning, soon after her arrival, he entered a room carrying a tray of breakfast for a guest and found her bound to the four corners of the bed, while her companion was taking a shower in the bathroom. Wasting no time he dropped his trouser and thrust his cock into her, screwing her quickly and yet sensuously, the rotation of his hips and the attention he paid to her breasts bringing her a swift but intense orgasm, so that when he withdrew she kissed him. He grinned at her and then was gone, leaving her client none the wiser when he returned to his captive a few minutes later.

After that Art would occasionally sneak into her room during the day, wakening her then rolling her onto her back, always marvelling at the way she would spread her legs at the sight of his stiff penis.

Lia grew to enjoy his visits; the sex was enjoyable and they became quite friendly, chatting idly about this and that. She learned about the Black Cat; how it was ruled with an iron fist by Helda along with a small clique of Bikers. How it was clandestinely advertised in the cities and among the aristocratic landowners who still remained behind their walled estates in the country. He showed her copies of the brochure that would be sent out regularly, containing the same information as the book in the foyer. He whispered to her the names of some of those who visited. Noblemen, heads of state, film and TV stars, all visited at some time or another. From him Lia began to learn a lot more about the clandestine world into which she had been plunged.

Then one evening came an event that would change everything. Lia had been waiting in her room for the usual summons. She felt fresh, her hair washed and groomed, her body recently bathed, and she stood before the mirror examining herself critically, but finding no fault. She heard the door open, and was surprised to see not the usual man in overalls to take her to her evening's companion, but Justine, another of the Black Cat's hostesses.

Justine was the girl featured in the brochure in leather with high-heeled boots, as she was dressed now, with fishnet stockings and suspenders, shiny leather bikini, the boots rolled over below the knees and a strange winged mask covering her eyes. The sight of her made Lia shrink back momentarily. They had never spoken and Lia was wary of her, with her cruel eyes and haughty air.

"Turn round," Justine barked. "Hands together."

Lia complied and felt cold handcuffs close about her wrists. A second pair secured her arms above the elbows. Then she was shoved through the doorway and along the hall. She wanted to ask where they were going, but Justine's detached air did not encourage questions. For a while she thought they were headed for the guestrooms, but then they took a turn and Lia realised with a shiver that they were approaching the dungeon.

She had heard of the dungeon from Art, but had not yet seen it. She knew it to be a special room set aside for those with particular tastes. According to Art it was sound-proofed to prevent any cries reaching the rest of the establishment.

They began to descend a flight of winding stairs, going further and further down. The walls were bare brick now, the only light coming from naked lightbulbs set into the walls at intervals. The smell was damp and musty and the stone steps felt cold beneath her bare feet. They came to a door, made of thick oak, with a great iron handle which creaked as Justine turned it.

The room was large and windowless, the walls bare brick, with iron rings from which hung chains. It was filled with ancient apparatus, the purpose of which Lia did not recognise, although the chains and shackles attached to most betrayed them as objects of torture. In one corner was a darkened alcove, above which harsh spotlights were mounted, shining blindingly so it was not possible to see what was inside. Lia was led to the middle of the room in the full glare of the lights.

"Very nice thank you, Justine."

Lia jumped when the voice came from the alcove. It was deep and rough with an uncultured accent, and somehow it seemed familiar to her. She searched her mind to try and remember where she had heard it before, but was unable to place it.

"Prepare her."

Justine undid the cuffs, and led her to a device that stood close to the alcove. It consisted of a padded bench about three feet high, standing on four legs, at the end of each a leather band. Lia was placed in front of it, her bare pubis resting against the leather padding. Her legs were spread and the leather bands buckled round her ankles. Justine bent her forward over the bench, stretching her arms down and fixing her wrists in a similar manner. A wide strap was pulled over her waist, holding her securely, unable even to struggle. She lay watching Justine as the girl selected a whip from the rack. It had a stout handle, with nine separate leather strands, each terminating in a tight knot.

Justine positioned herself behind her captive, dangling the thongs down between her buttocks so that the tips ran lightly across her sex lips, making Lia shudder with the sensation.

"Right, punish her. Make the little bitch scream."

The beating was the worst Lia had ever received. Justine brought the whip down with unbelievable force, each knotted tip stinging with terrible ferocity. Justine operated systematically, working her way from Lia's toned buttocks up to her shoulders, then down again over the backs of her legs to her knees, each blow striking with terrible force, Lia screaming, begging for mercy.

"Enough!"

Just when Lia felt she would pass out the order came and the blows ceased. For a moment the room was quiet, the silence broken only by the panting of Justine and the sobbing of Lia.

The man behind the lights spoke again. "Chain her to the bench."

Justine worked swiftly, undoing the straps, then dragging the girl across to a metal frame, like a short table with a wooden surface. She forced Lia onto her back, ignoring her groans as she felt the wood on her wounded skin. A strap went across her belly and her feet were attached to shackles that hung from above, so that tightening the chain forced Lia's legs up and apart, stretching her sex open. Another strap was tightened below her breasts and her hands were manacled together and pulled behind her head, where they were fastened to a ring on the wooden surface. Thus she hung, her backside suspended in mid-air over the edge of the bench, her sex raised, totally accessible.

"Well done," said the voice. "You may go now."

Justine gave a slight bow then was gone, leaving Lia with her invisible master.

"Well," there was an edge to the voice that made Lia's blood run cold, "we meet again."

"Who... who are you?"

"Surely you remember. It's not that long ago."

"I... I can't..."

"Perhaps a closer look will help." There was the scraping of a chair, then she saw a figure emerge from the alcove. She strained to make him out, the silhouette broad and muscular, the head bald and shining. Then he was standing beside her, the light on his face, and suddenly the memory came back of a squalid room in a dingy hostel in the city. Of an exercise bench, and a honed knife handle.

It was the watchman!

Lia let out a gasp of disbelief. Surely it wasn't possible? How could he possibly have found her? But it was definitely him. Her heart sank as she saw the two ugly scars, one on his forehead, the other down his temple, and remembered how he had come by them.

"Remember me now? Slightly worse for wear, I'll admit, but not as dead as you thought I was."

"But how...?"

"How did I find you? Well, that wasn't too difficult. You left quite an interesting trail. You really should be a little more discreet. It was this that put me onto you."

He held up a magazine. Lia stared at it. Her eyes widened. The cover image was a girl, completely naked, her legs apart, her sex thrust forward, her hands stretched back over her head so they rested on a mirror, which perfectly reflected her backside. It was a picture of her in the diner!

He sneered down at her discomfort. "It was a bit of a giveaway, having your photo plastered over the front page of a porny magazine that's on display in every newsagent in the city. The girls from the factory were most shocked, but that didn't stop them buying a copy. And it's a good thing. It gets even better inside."

To Lia's shame he began turning the pages in front of her. There she was, being searched intimately by the officer, although he benefitted by having his face pixelated out. There were others too: being whipped in the pool room, the photo taken through the open door; standing on the table, her face and breasts covered with sperm; shots with the bottle rammed deep into her vagina, an expression of rapt eroticism on her face; then still more outside being hosed down by the barmaid. Her face reddened as he began to read the text.

"...Not content with fucking the cop and giving the deputy the blowjob of his life, this sexy little minx gave a display with a whisky bottle that would have made an experienced whore blush with shame, having one of the noisiest and most public orgasms ever recorded in this magazine." He grinned.

"They say these pictures are pinned up in every locker in the clothes factory. Even the boss keeps a copy in his bottom drawer. Well, after that it wasn't too difficult to find you. I asked a few questions around the truckers' depot, heard you'd joined the Bikers, then managed to get hold of a brochure for this place. It makes you sound very tempting."

"What do you want?"

"Well, first of all to see you thoroughly thrashed. And I still haven't had that fuck you promised me, Number Seventeen." He reached behind him and pulled something from his belt. Lia shrank back as she recognised the knife.

"Remember having this up you? Yes, I'm sure you do. Well this time, Number Seventeen, you're going to feel the other end. I'm going to make you pay for these scars by giving you a few of your own. But first I think you need a little more whipping. Let's see what Justine can do when she really tries."

He crossed to a wall, where he pulled on a rope. A bell was heard to ring somewhere, then he returned to stand over the terrified girl. Behind him the door opened. "Nice and hard this time," he said, without turning. "And let's see you make it good."

It wasn't till the footsteps were right behind him that he realised something was amiss, and by then it was too late. The iron ball swung on the end of its chain and came down on the back of his head with a sickening crunch. He toppled to the floor and lay still. Lia's mouth dropped open.

It was Thorkil!

He smiled down at her. "It seems I'm in the nick of time once again."

She gasped. "But how, why...?"

"Tell you later. We've got to get out of here." He began undoing the shackles that held her, releasing first her legs, then her arms. When she was able to stand she threw herself into his arms.

"Oh Thorkil," she sobbed, "I thought I'd never see you again."

He wrapped his arms around her, holding her close. "You don't get rid of me that easily," he quipped, easing her arms from around him. "Come on, let's get out of here."

Grabbing her by the hand he made for the door. He inched it open, peering through the crack. "OK," he said, "let's go."

He led her up the winding staircase, pausing at the top to check the corridor. It was empty. They set off, taking a left turn down a passage Lia was unfamiliar with. It led them into one of the back corridors where the working quarters were. Thorkil led the way, showing a knowledge of the building that surprised her. She could only assume someone had given him the information beforehand.

At last they came to a door that led out to the grounds. Once again Thorkil was cautious, checking the way was clear before venturing outside.

They made their way across the lawns, keeping as close to the hedges as possible. Thorkil led her by the hand, looking about all the time as they dodged from bush to bush. At last they were in sight of the main gates. Like the fence that surrounded the Black Cat it was very tall, the top lined with barbed wire.

"How are we going to get out?" whispered Lia.

"I've got to get to the mechanism that controls the gate and try to find out how it works. That'll take a little time. I'll need a diversion, and that's where you come in."

"Me?"

"Yes. You've got to lure the three guards away from the gatehouse office. There's a small restroom behind. If you can get them in there I'll be able to get the gate open. Think you can do it?"

Lia swallowed, fighting down the fear, but it was the least she could do after he'd risked so much. "I'll do it," she said, then planting a kiss on his cheek, she took a deep breath and walked towards the gatehouse.

The building was a low brick built structure, with wide windows overlooking the driveway and the great gates. The area about it was floodlit, and as Lia approached she was aware of her total exposure in the harshness of the illumination. She strode up to the door, knocked once then opened it and stepped inside.

The room, like the outside, was brightly lit and smelled of cigarette smoke. On one side was the mechanism that worked the gates. Next to that was a large white board covered with writing in felt-tip; some sort of roster, she guessed. The three men were sitting around a table playing cards. They gazed open-mouthed at the interloper.

Lia leaned back against the door with studied nonchalance, placing her feet apart and putting her hands on her hips. "You guys got any ointment?"

"What?"

"Ointment. You know, something to stop the pain. That bitch Justine just gave me a thrashing. Just look at my poor bum." She walked over to where they sat, and turning round bent over, displaying her welted behind to them. "You got something you could rub into that?" she asked.

The men were taken aback, though clearly delighted by what they saw. Lia turned, standing deliberately close to the nearest of the three so that her sex was only inches from his face. "I'll tell you what always works after I've been whipped," she continued. "Spunk. A good dollop of fresh spunk rubbed into my arse. And on my tits. The skin gets so dry, you see. Feel how dry my tits are." She leant over the man, shoving her breasts at him. He reached out tentatively and felt them, squeezing gently.

"Th-they feel OK to me," he said.

"You think so? What do you think?" She went around the table, allowing all three to caress her breasts in turn, her blatant behaviour beginning to excite her, her nipples responding to the caresses of the men by hardening into erect buds.

"Jeez," she purred seductively, "having you guys feel my tits is turning me on. My cunt's sopping. Isn't there somewhere more comfortable we could go?"

The men looked at one another. "The restroom?" suggested one.

"What about the gate?" said another.

"Sod the bloody gate. They won't be coming out for hours. Let's go for it. About time we had some fun too."

They jumped to their feet, grabbing Lia by the arms and dragging her through a door at the back of the office. The restroom was sparsely furnished, having two beds and a couple of armchairs. It was on one of the beds that they dropped her.

Lia lay back, opening her legs as she felt a hand sliding up her thighs and probing her wet vagina. She gasped with genuine pleasure as she felt fingers slip inside her. The other two were positioned on either side of her, caressing her breasts. She closed her eyes as she felt a mouth close over each of her nipples, her hips gyrating against the fingers probing deep within her. She reached out for the man who's hand was giving her so much pleasure, her fingers scrabbling with his belt then sliding down his fly, reaching inside for his cock.

She held it in her hand, working the foreskin back and forth, feeling it harden and grow beneath her deft touch. The attention to her breasts and sex was making her writhe about on the bed, moaning. She clutched the stiff rod in her hand, pulling him closer.

"Fuck me," she sighed, totally absorbed in pleasure. "Fuck me. Fuck me." She felt his hand withdraw as he manoeuvred himself over her, then his penis was pressing into her. She let out a cry of delight as she felt it penetrate, shoving its way into her as she eased her legs apart to accommodate it. Deeper and deeper it went, its thickness stretching the walls of her vagina, the friction producing a delightful sensation within her hot sex.

He rammed himself fully inside her and began the slow rhythm of intercourse, driving his hips against her. The other two were still sucking her breasts, their saliva dribbling down into her cleavage and trickling from her torso.

The pumping of the cock between her legs increased in tempo as the man's arousal grew. Lia thrashed back and forth under the onslaught, moaning as she felt her lust rising. She reached out on either side, tearing at the flies of the other two, anxious to feel their stiff cocks in her hands. She found both simultaneously and began masturbating them urgently, her hands working their foreskins up and down in rhythm with the cock that filled her vagina, her orgasm approaching.

Then a new sound met her ears. It was a powerful motorcycle being revved just outside the gatehouse. With a start she was brought back to the reality of the situation. Thorkil; he must have opened the gates and was now waiting for her.

With a supreme effort of will Lia released the cocks in her hands, and with a heave rolled the man on top of her over so he fell from the bed, his cock slipping from within her. In the same movement she was on her feet and running for the door. A hand grabbed at her ankle but she shook it free, leaving the three behind her cursing as they struggled to pull up their pants from round their ankles.

Lia was through the gatehouse and outside where Thorkil was waiting. She jumped behind him on the throbbing machine and he dropped the clutch. She had to cling tightly to him as the bike roared off. They were away, Thorkil racing up through the gears with Lia's arms wrapped around him, her insides convulsing with the proximity of her orgasm.

The bike bumped and slid along the rugged road as she peered anxiously back, searching for any tell-tale lights of pursuers. Eventually they were leaning over hard as they swept onto the highway, and the Black Cat was receding fast into the distance.

They continued on down the highway for some fifteen minutes before Lia felt the machine begin to slow. Then they were back on a dirt track, snaking through a dense forest.

Thorkil rode on until they were well out of sight of the road, then he switched off, the machine gliding to a stop in a small grassy clearing. He dismounted and helped Lia off. He held her in a passionate embrace, their lips pressed together in a hungry kiss.

When at last he released her she leaned gratefully against him, enjoying the closeness of his body.

"How did you know I was in danger?"

"I have my spies. I took the trouble to find out who you were and what you were running from. It wasn't difficult. The little incident in the hostel made a few of the less reputable papers. After that I found out the watchman had been making enquiries of the truck drivers, and that he was going to the Black Cat. Then I had some help from a guy who works there; young fellow called Art. I think you know him."

Lia blushed at the mention of Art's name, wondering how much Thorkil knew about their relationship.

"He told me tonight was the night, so I thought, since I was coming anyhow, I'd better make sure you were still alive when I found you."

"You were coming anyway?"

"You didn't think I'd leave you there, did you?"

"But the auction. Surely I belong to Helda? Isn't that the Bikers' code?"

"Except for the fact that it turns out Helda's people started a fire which prevented me from attending the auction. That's why I wasn't there in time."

"So, you mean I can be yours?"

"Once I've squared a few things with Vargo, yes. Meanwhile I think you need taking into safekeeping."

"Oh, Thorkil!" She flung her arms around him again, hugging him tight and covering his face with kisses. Then she was on her knees, undoing his pants, anxious to taste him.

His cock was stiff and proud. She held it in her hands marvelling at its sculptured shape and size. She took it hungrily into her mouth, sucking hard while her fingers caressed his hefty balls. But he reached down and lifted her, laid her on the saddle of his machine, her arms stretched behind her head, a hand on each of the throttle grips, her legs tucked back so that her feet rested on the rear footrests. He grasped her thighs and she felt him enter her for the first time. Lia cried out with happiness as he thrust his hot, hungry organ into her vagina.

Now she truly was a Biker's Girl!

The Biker's Girl Trilogy

Biker's Girl 2 - On the Run

Once the door had closed the guard turned to look at her captive. "Such a pretty little thing," she murmured. She lifted the spear so the metal brushed Lia's cheek.

Lia stayed perfectly still; the point was razor sharp. The guard moved the weapon, sliding the edge down Lia's throat, making the hapless girl tremble. She slid it down her front and over her swelling breasts, just scratching her nipples, the sensation making them harden. The guard smiled and continued to tease them, the edge of the steel sending a tremor through Lia's body.

In this second **Biker's Girl** book Lia, our beautifully submissive damsel in distress, again remains totally naked throughout, stumbling from one erotic mishap to another, pursued and hunted by numerous devious dominants and being regularly punished in all sorts of imaginative ways.

Biker's Girl 3 - Decent to Debauchery

Lia straightened, rubbing her bum, the tears trickling down her face. She'd had much worse beatings since she became a slave to the Bikers, but almost never one so humiliating; the stinging in her bottom eclipsed by her extreme embarrassment as she glanced around at the leering customers.

Submissive damsel in distress Lia's sexual adventures come to an erotic climax in **Biker's Girl 3 - Descent to Debauchery**!

And both books are available as paperbacks at **AMAZON**.

www.ingramcontent.com/pod-product-compliance
Lightning Source LLC
Chambersburg PA
CBHW070753120626

46557CB00002B/581